Eileen,

MW01127859

BEVERLY PRESTON

Shayla's Story

Always be
sinfully sexy!,

Beverly Preston

This book is a work of fiction. All characters, organizations, and events portrayed in this novel are either products of the author's imagination or are used fictitiously.

Copyright © 2013 by Beverly Preston
ISBN: 1490470042
ISBN 13: 978-1490470047

Cover image by Rob Lang.
http://www.roblangimages.com/

Cover designed by Linda Boulanger
www.TellTaleBookCovers.weebly.com

Visit Beverly at www.beverlypreston.com

"I devoured this book, even when I tried to put it down it consumed my thoughts! Captivated by Shayla and charmed by John, *Shayla's Story* will have you engrossed and yearning for more."
– Diana (Dame) at Confessions of a Book Heaux

Titles by Bestselling Author

BEVERLY PRESTON

The Mathews/Clemmins Family Series:

No More Wasted Time

Shayla's Story

~ More from The Mathews/Clemmins Family ~
Series in early 2014

www.beverlypreston.com

To Don – my Richard, my Tommy, my John
I love you

ACKNOWLEDGMENTS

To Don, my husband who loves me endlessly, thanks for cooking more often, putting up with a messy house and sacrificing a few date nights while I took the time to write.

My youngest daughter, thank you for making wonderful dinners, you may truly be a chef one day.

My four kids, thanks for allowing me to bounce questions off of you, no matter how absurd. Your input proves to be invaluable to me.

Caylee, my oldest daughter, words cannot express the gratitude I have for all of the time spent helping me with final line edits. Even though the hours proved to be grueling, I absolutely loved every minute. You are awesome! You are my rock, my best friend!

To my family and friends who supported me in my endeavors, gave me words of encouragement and showed up with wine at the perfect time, your support and friendship are priceless. Sandy Mohn, Sherrie Lee, Karen Collins, Jewel Peck, and Lynette Owens, thanks for your support ladies!

Rob Lang and Linda Boulanger for providing the photograph and design work to create a gorgeous cover.

Paul Rega, thank you for enlightening me in the art of self-promotion. Go team Pay It Forward!

I would also like to thank Natascha at SPJ Editing, my friend and editor.

Ellen DeGeneres, I hope you read this someday; without you there would be no dream.

To everyone who is falling in love with The Mathews/Clemmins Family, I cannot thank you enough for your patience, support and words of encouragement.

CHAPTER ONE

Clumps of firmly packed sand fell from Shayla's feet, leaving a trail of wet footprints across the parking lot. Droplets from her ponytail and wetsuit evaporated on contact with the warm concrete sidewalk.

Shayla reached back, tugging on the zipper pull at the nape of her neck, exposing her bare shoulders to the warmth of the California sunrays slipping through the morning haze. Stopping to adjust her surfboard, she gave a cordial nod to the group of hard-bodied surfers changing beneath the towels wrapped around their waists.

Record-breaking November temperatures rejuvenated the typically tranquil morning into a bustling day at the beach. Families loaded down with bulky coolers, beach chairs, floppy hats and SPF 50 rushed to stake a claim on a blanket size piece of prime Malibu beach real estate.

Every day at 10:00am came the changing of the tide; big swells that drew the early morning lineup of surfers mellowed, leaving ideal waves for body boarders to enjoy.

Shayla trekked up the hill heading for home. Sounds of the weakening surf grew faint, replaced by the croon of mocking birds taking up residence in the giant palm trees that lined the quaint, established neighborhood. She extended neighborly hellos to the routine dog-walkers and exercise enthusiasts out for their morning run.

Shayla rounded the corner, and a surprised smile etched across her lips as she caught a glimpse of the familiar silver sedan parked in her driveway. Her pace quickened and she anxiously trotted down the pavestone driveway. Shayla hadn't seen Mat in over two weeks, other than dropping by campaign headquarters to deliver lunch and a quick peck on the cheek. He'd barely found time to answer her goodnight phone call.

She fumbled one-handedly with the latch on the redwood gate. Propping her board against the house, she ducked into the outdoor shower hidden within the lush foliage at the back of her house. Shimmying out of her wetsuit and bikini, she impatiently washed off the remainder of gritty sand and saltwater, replacing it with the sweet scent of honeysuckle body-wash and shampoo.

Mathew Huntston was the son of Margret Huntston, Mayor of the affluent city of View Point. After two terms as acting Mayor, she set her sights on bigger and brighter lights: the Governorship of the state of California. She had the reputation of a feminine liberal, but many perceived her as cold and ambitious. Shayla simply thought of her as the potential intimidating future mother-in-law from hell.

Mat hadn't popped the question, but he'd brought up *somedays* and *forevers* on more than one occasion. At the moment, Shayla was simply more interested in *right now*. She hoped to take advantage of a private moment whenever they got the chance. November marked the beginning of a yearlong campaign. The grueling schedule and highly publicized campaign would be daunting.

Shayla wrung the excess water from her long blonde hair and wrapped a towel around her. The mouthwatering aroma of breakfast hit her before she even made it through the back door.

Mat stood in front of the stove dressed in grey slacks and a light blue dress shirt. Steam drifted from a kettle as he poured boiling water into her favorite mug on the counter.

"Hey." She padded barefoot behind him resting her hand on his firm shoulder. "This is a nice surprise."

Mat turned to face her, placing a kiss of affection on top her head. "Me or the breakfast?"

"Both," she simmered. Shayla teetered on her toes, raising her lips toward his. Slipping her fingers into the folds of the towel, she began to disrobe. "I didn't expect to see you until tonight."

Mat briefly pressed his lips to hers before clasping hold of her delicate hands and drawing them to his lips. "I can't stay. I have to get back to work."

Her hopes of spending the morning in bed squashed, she slumped, resting her forehead against to his chest in disappointment.

A gorgeous arrangement of vibrant lilac iris and sweet-smelling magnolia blossoms beaconed from the center of the breakfast nook table. "He seems to have outdone himself this time."

Shayla twisted her neck, following Mat's gaze to the stunning bouquet. Shayla's uncle made a thoughtful habit of sending her flowers for any and all special occasions. "They are beautiful and they stand for good luck."

"And I just bet they smell good too."

"You know, it's not a competition."

"I'm just glad I brought you breakfast instead of flowers." He cupped her chin, flashing a charade of a smile. "And I have something for you to wear tonight."

"I'd rather just wear you tonight."

Mat personified the term Classic Male Americana; everything from his sandy blonde hair and trim defined physique, to the predictable turtleneck sweater he'd wear that evening. He could lavish her with extravagant gifts, but all she truly yearned for was quality time spent together as a couple.

He pulled a white box with the initials HW from his pocket and set it in her hand. "I thought these would be the perfect accessory for you to wear at the gala."

Mat lifted the lid, exposing a pair of gorgeous drop earrings.

Shayla traced the tip of her finger over the delicate strand of brilliant diamonds and rubies linked to form the shape of a heart. She smiled, touched by his attention to detail. The *Have a Heart Foundation* was Shayla's favorite charity and tonight was the *Bare Your Soul* extravaganza.

"They're beautiful," she whispered softly, wrapping her arms around his waist.

Mat stood aloof, patting her back mechanically.

Mat was *not* a big hugger. Displaying emotion through the warmth of physical connection of any kind seemed unacceptable in the Huntston family. Shayla suspected Mrs. Huntston thought of sentiment as weakness, a politian's Achilles' Heel. Every time she greeted Mat or his family with even the slightest embrace, it was like wrapping her arms around an ironing board. She learned quickly to abandon her typical greeting of a comforting hug, replacing it with a proper handshake or civil nod of the head.

Peering down at the gift, she narrowed her eyes as a foreseeable notion climbed into her head. "You *are* still coming to the gala with me tonight, aren't you?"

"Of course." He scoffed as if she were acting impractical, resting his hands firmly on both shoulders. "Tonight is one of Los Angeles' biggest social events of the year. I'd never miss it."

"Of course," she repeated disheartened, dropping her arms at her side. "Voters. And here I thought maybe you were attending the gala to raise awareness for heart disease."

He wiggled the breakfast-to-go box with Lo-coMoco written across the top as if it were a peace offering. "I'm *attending* to support my girlfriend."

The delicious aroma of her favorite breakfast, a LocoMoco surf bowl, eased her irritancy when hunger took over. Sounds of appreciation swelled from her throat.

"Yumm." She pulled out two forks and handed one to Mat, eagerly digging into the layers of brown rice, turkey burger, salsa, three egg whites and a pinch of sprinkle cheese.

"Unfortunately––" he shook his head, passing on breakfast and setting his fork back on the counter " –I *do* have an important meeting, a dinner meeting, so I'm going –"

"What?" She choked on a mouth full of food. "Seriously, Mat?"

Unable to mask her anger and disappointment, Shayla nearly lobbed the bowl on the counter. "I'm announcing this year's recipient of the Humanitarian Award! Tonight's a huge honor for me! Why—"

"I'll be there. I'm simply going to be a little late. Cecil Marsh is one of our biggest contributors."

Her mouth dropped open. "Cecil is one of your mother's good friends—"

"Cecil endorsed *my father* until he had no choice but to walk away after my father's affair became national news. His support is essential for my mother's campaign. We've already leaked it to the media and my presence shows a strong united force."

"I've already arranged for a car to pick you up. I promise to make it up to you after the gala." He flashed his infamous smile known for soothing her irritancy.

Her gaze shifted out the window toward the ocean. They'd already had this discussion several times. She understood the campaign would be his number one priority, but he'd promised to support her at the *Have a Heart* fundraiser.

Each of them had busy careers, which required unwavering loyalty. Shayla worked diligently as her uncle's personal assistant for six years, not including the four years he spent coaching her for the position while attending college. Her job was most often filled a forty hour plus work week, but at times required her attention twelve hours a day seven days a week.

Shayla admired Mat's steadfast devotion to his family and job. However, her uncle would never purposely sabotage an important event to drive a wedge between her and Mat.

Margret Huntston would.

She released a heavy exhale, calming her frustration while she collected her thoughts.

Mat jiggled her fingers, waiting for a response.

"You don't need to send a car. I'll just drive. I should get there early anyway." She didn't need to arrive early, but it rolled out of her mouth, wanting to keep the peace and her agitation from boiling over. The last thing she needed today was another round in the on-going debate about how little time they spent together. "Thank you for the earrings."

"I'll be there," he assured, heading toward the front door.

"I hope so," she said somberly, reaching for the doorknob. "I make the announcement at 9:30pm."

"I won't be late." Mat kissed her cheek and jaunted down the front steps.

Traipsing into the kitchen, Shayla dug into her surf bowl. Daydreaming out the window, she wondered if he'd really show up on time. Judging past performances, Mat would be late. She believed in being perpetually punctual and Mat was always fashionably late.

The buzzing of her cell phone brought her into reality. Seeing her best friends face flash across the screen, she answered, "Hello?"

"Hey! I'm so glad I caught you," Carrie Ann babbled anxiously on the other end of the line. "I figured you'd be on your board this morning."

"I just walked in from the beach a few minutes ago. How's set up going?"

"Great. Actually, I'm not there. I left the other members in charge so I can finish the calendar shoot.

Which is why I'm calling," Carrie Ann spewed in a caffeine-fueled rush of words. As a member of the Advisory Board to the *Have a Heart Foundation*, Carrie Ann created the *Bare Your Soul* calendar. "I was thinking, you should come over here and get your hair and makeup done for tonight."

Shayla didn't spend much time on her hair, keeping it all one length and naturally blonde. She dreaded the extra fuss of hair and makeup that came with attending charity events, movie openings and any other red carpet extravaganzas requiring more than a blow-dryer and flat-iron. "Are you sure? That would be awesome!"

"Ha! I knew you'd be happy. You owe me." Playful sarcasm filtered through her amusement.

"Would you prefer your traditional rich creamy vanilla latte or the holiday favorite, pumpkin spice?" Shayla mocked in her best sales pitch voice. "Whip? Or no whip?"

"No more coffee for me. I've drunk enough caffeine to organize three charity events. I'll be switching to Vodka if my day gets any worse," Carrie Ann taunted with a grumble.

"What's the problem? Too many creative thinking caps in one room?"

"Something like that. Hurry up and get over here so I can vent in detail."

"Try to hold off on the Vodka until after dinner."

"Yeah…okay," Carrie Ann teased doubtfully, her tone sounding calmer already. "Speaking of dinner. What time are you and Mat arriving tonight?"

"I take it back, I'll bring the shaker and glasses. Let's start now." Shayla's humor soured and she cleared the agitation from her throat. "I'm flying so-lo."

Silence.

"Oh boy," Carrie Ann finally said. "Bring your gown. We'll go together."

Her spirits lifted. "That sounds like a fantastic idea. I'll be there in a half hour."

The extreme beach house Carrie Ann borrowed from her real estate acquaintance for her photo shoot left Shayla speechless as she pulled up to the grand driveway.

She entered the code Carrie Ann gave her and the regal iron gate creaked open with grandeur slowness. Following directions, she parked her car in the garage and gathered her things. Carrying a small overnight bag and her dress, she stepped into the elevator.

The doors parted when she reached the ground level.

"Wow," she said in astonishment.

Shayla ventured into the dramatic entrance at a turtle's pace, taking in the stark modern sophistication of the home. Glass and light filled the house with sunshine, illuminating the art hanging singularly on each white wall. The slapping of her sandals echoed against the bare concrete floors as she cautiously made her way across a bridge floating above a magnificent fish aquarium.

She peered down into a massive tank filled with vibrant artificial coral and colorful fish. "It's like an art museum for fish."

Familiar voices swept through the house, carried in with a cool moist breeze and the sounds of the crashing surf.

"Hello?" she called out.

Carrie Ann peeked in from outside the open

doorway at the back of the house. "Pretty cool, isn't it?"

"I'll say." Shayla scanned over the contemporary sculpture made of scrap metal taking on the shape of a woman standing in the breeze with her hair blowing in long wisps. The large piece encompassed the entire a corner of the living room.

Carrie Ann greeted her with a quick squeeze. "The private after-party starts right after the gala, but I'm keeping it low key."

Her fair skin and pixie cut accentuated the mischievous sparkle in her emerald eyes, but most people only made it as far as her cleavage. She unapologetically embraced her full figured curves in a city known for its paper-thin image.

"I'll have to pass. Mat and I have *plans*." Heat climbed to her cheeks and Shayla grinned apologetically. She dropped her head back and lifted her hands skyward with fingers extended fully. "Finally! A night alone."

"Aw, you poor thing." Carrie Ann pouted impishly. "You *still* haven't gotten laid? What's it been? Two weeks?"

"Try almost four!" Shayla opened her eyes wide with painful protest. "He dropped by this morning to give me a pair of earrings to wear tonight. I thought I was going to tackle him right there in the kitchen, but before I could even get my towel off, he left."

"I told you. You need to take care of yourself." Carrie Ann's wiggled her brows while sliding her fingers down her abs and grabbing hold of her crotch as if she were dirty dancing on MTV. "*Pleasure* yourself."

Her spirit shone as vibrant as her flame red

hair.

Shayla giggled then frowned in frustration. "It's not the same."

Nodding in agreement, Carrie Ann taunted in a prim and proper tone, "Besides, *Mathew Huntston* would never get down and dirty in the kitchen."

A grey seagull swooped down and landed on the terrace, momentarily capturing their attention with a harsh squawking, scavenging for any remnants left behind.

"What did he gift you this time?" Carrie Ann extended her hand, palm up, fingers wiggling with curiosity. "I know *you* could care less about material items, but I'd like to get some enjoyment out of Mat's latest donation to the *I'm sorry I fucked up* gift box."

Shayla did a once around the world eye roll as she rummaged blindly through her bag, handing the box to Carrie Ann. Not bothering to wait for the ooh's and aah's, she kicked off her sandals and moseyed onto the terrace perched on a jagged rock cove above the private beach below.

When Shayla first arrived on her uncle's doorstep a few weeks after graduating high school, she found it nearly impossible to fit in. There was no shortage of wealth under the glamorous lights of Los Angeles and her famous uncle ranked at the top of the list. Tom Clemmins was an A-list actor with a blockbuster career spanning nearly thirty years, but he still managed modesty. Lavish homes and extravagant cars were as common as the coffee house on every corner. The obsessive strive for the perception of flawlessness made her very uncomfortable.

The sunshine warmed the terrace beneath her toes as she leaned over the railing and gaped down at the secluded beach below. A natural bend in the outcropping of rocks created a small private beach, restricted from public access on both sides. Tony, a well-known celebrity photographer, climbed the switchback steps notched into the rocks, leaving his tripod and camera equipment set up on the white sand below. His makeup artist/stylist, Rachel, trotted up the stairs behind him.

Tony's shoulder length hair, bleached blonde from the California sunshine fell around his face. He glanced up and smiled, tucking the long layers behind his ear. "Hello, sweetheart."

"Hey, Tony." She extended her hand.

His cool fingers encircled hers with a soft pat.

"Where is everybody?" Shayla questioned.

Tony's mouth opened then closed. A surprised glaze washed over his face and his gaze drifted beyond Shayla.

Carrie Ann walked up behind her, clearing her throat. "Ummm, we need to talk about that."

Shayla's stare darted between them. Judging by the terrified looks on their faces, she assumed something was wrong. "Oh, man. Did I miss it? Please tell me I don't have to fix my own hair?"

Rachel waved hello and buzzed right past, appearing to be on a mission. "No, I'm ready whenever you are, Shayla. I'll just…wait for you in the hair and makeup salon."

"They have a salon?"

"And a theater and gym too." Carrie Ann wrapped her arm around Shayla's shoulder. "I need you to do me a huge favor."

Pleading saturated her voice.

Realizing the severity in her reaction, Shayla narrowed her eyes, "Sure. Of course, what do you need?"

"I need you to bare your soul."

CHAPTER TWO

"Hell no! I am not posing naked for the *Bare Your Soul Calendar*!" Shayla screeched, shirking away from Carrie Ann's arm draped over her shoulder, which now felt more like the clutches of entrapment.

"You won't be totally naked." She trotted into the kitchen and returned with a heart-shaped foam board covered in gorgeous crimson satin fabric and a wide airy ribbon tied in a stunning bow. "See! Nothing will be exposed—"

"You can't be serious. I'm won't pose naked and besides, no one even knows who I am. The calendar is filled each year with celebrities, rock stars,"—Shayla posed like a super model, mimicked a rock star jamming on his guitar then tossed her arms in the air with bent elbows mimicking a field goal—"and athletes! Not people like me!"

"Oh please! A lot of people know who you are and you're the epitome of all those people combined. You're the quintessential poster child for fitness. Hell, you could represent the State of California in one of their campaign ads to attract—"

Shayla raised her hand. "What happened? Who was supposed to be here?"

Carrie Ann shot Tony a fleeting glance, obviously searching for any assistance.

He swiftly dropped his view to the ground, brushing the sand off one bare foot with the other.

Carrie Ann paused in reluctance.

"Oh great." Shayla flopped back onto a lounge sofa big enough for ten people. "Just exactly *who* are you asking me to replace?"

"Babs was—"

"Babs!" Shayla lurched to her feet. "Are you kidding? You're asking *me* to fill in for Babs?"

She clutched her petite breasts then held her hands in front of her chest as if holding two generous watermelons. "That's—that's, that's like comparing Nemo to a whale shark or a Mini Cooper to a stretch limo or like—"

"I've rescheduled this photo shoot three times for her. I knew better than to depend on that bitch, but the other board members outvoted me. That woman is completely unstable!"

"Are you seriously asking me to fill in for a notorious sex symbol?" Her tummy fluttered with nerves. "She a bombshell! A pin up girl! A—"

"She's a fucking high maintenance diva, a drama queen! That's what she is," Carrie Ann protested, throwing her hands in the air. "It's not my fault she woke up this morning with one of her best assets flatter than a pancake! It happened yesterday and she didn't bother calling me until fifteen minutes before she was supposed to be here. Not to mention she was half-lit and crying hysterically, complaining her world had ended. 'What are all my fans around the world going to say?'"

Shayla made a painful face, repositioning her hands in front of her chest to the image she now stuck in her head. One perfect bazooka gum bubble at its finest, the other burst in a spatter.

"It's okay! Don't worry, Shayla," Carrie Ann continued in a rant, hands flailing and head bobbing sassily. "Everything is hunky dory over in Bab's world. The surgeon is going to replace both her breasts to a new and improved *larger* implant."

Shayla mouthed, *bigger?*

"Then she had the nerve to suggest we re-schedule the shoot in a few months." Carrie Ann shook her head and took a deep breath. Tears of frustration filled her eyes.

Shayla was taken aback. She'd never seen Carrie Ann cry once in the last ten years.

Carrie Ann befriended her in college, when she moved to Malibu. Their personalities were as diverse as their upbringing. Carrie Ann grew up in Beverly Hills, with neighbors ranging from rock stars to film producers. Shayla was raised in a podunk town in Kentucky where the only thing her neighbors were known for was a good dose of moonshine. Carrie Ann never judged her, and their friendship remained unwavering over the years.

"Look just hear me out. Please —"

"Okay."

Her friend squinted warily. "Okay?"

"Yes, all right. I'll do it."

Carrie Ann leapt from the sofa, throwing her arms around Shayla. "Oh, God, thank you! You have no idea how much you're saving my ass."

"You owe me."

Tony clasped his hands loudly and entwined his fingers as if his prayers had been answered.

Shayla pointed her finger at Tony. "No peeking! I don't want to hear one joke about this, Tony. Not one!"

She'd known Tony for a few years through

social contacts and he'd photographed her uncle more than once, but posing nude in front of him would be one of the most uncomfortable things she'd ever done in her life.

Tony caressed her arm. Each stroke came with a positive reassurance. "Sweetheart, I've seen more ta-ta's than Hugh. I'm simply happy to get back to work. You're going to do just fine. I promise to make it as painless and tasteful as possible."

"Owe you?" Carrie Ann chimed in, her gratitude already checked at the door as she waved her finger in the air. "I believe we are now officially even. I forget. Who was it that set you up with Mat? Oh, that's right. Me!"

A rough bark of laughter from Tony drew her attention. "What?" Shayla insisted.

"Oh, nothing." Tony shrugged nonchalantly, but a smug glint of humor gleamed in his eyes. "I just wish I could be the preverbal fly on the wall when you inform Mrs. Huntston you posed nude."

Out of the corner of her eye, Carrie Ann gave a blunt chop off your head sign to Tony.

Shayla sucked in a shallow breath. "Shit."

She hadn't considered the ramifications of posing naked for the calendar and what they might cause Mat. His mother would undoubtedly see it as scandalous and a potential threat to her campaign. Her nervousness turned to trepidation. She and Mat had each grown up being controlled by their parents. He reveled in it, living by certain standards and constantly seeking his mother's approval. Shayla escaped on a Greyhound bus and needed years of therapy.

"It's for charity, Shayla. Just think of how much money you're raising for heart disease." Her best friend pulled out all the stops. "You're saving lives. How can she argue with that?"

"Oh, believe me, she'll find a way."

****

Shayla emerged from the salon a product of natural radiance. Her skin glistened with a new sun kissed glow, but her anxiety floundered between awkward and mortification. She had a difficult time controlling her nervous giggles. After thirty minutes posing precariously on a rock on the beach while clasping onto the heart for dear life, Tony called a break.

He reassured her sweetly, trying to calm her angst. "Relax, sweetheart. You don't have to frolic in the sand, just let go of your inhibitions. Loosen your stance and stare seductively into the camera."

Time ticked by and sun began etching its way beyond the mid afternoon point and he still hadn't snapped the ideal shot. Agitation wore deep-notched groves between his brows. "This isn't working. You don't look comfortable. You're too uptight, I need you feel natural and at ease, Shayla."

"I'm not comfortable! I'm completely out of my element. How the hell am I supposed to look natural when I've got sand wedged up my ass and my cheeks hurt from smiling?" She kicked the sand in frustration.

Rachel came in for another round of spritzing. Her loose wet strands of hair fell around her shoulders and an ocean breeze sent a chill over her arms.

"I'm usually on a surfboard, Tony. Not naked!"

His brows rose with new interest. "Carrie Ann!" he shouted.

She had long since retreated inside. Shayla

assumed it was to avoid the catastrophe unfolding in front of her. The *Bare Your Soul Calendar* was her personal baby and this year marked her five-year anniversary. She poked her head over the balcony. "Yeah?"

"Go find a surf board! They gotta have a dozen or so lying around this mansion!"

Moments later, she pranced down the steps, boobs bouncing, surfboard in hand and a hopeful smile beaming across her face. She wedged the tip of the board into the soft sand. "Here you go. Great idea."

"Now," Tony demanded with bolstered positive encouragement, "wade out about ten yards, straddle your board and smile."

She'd expected him to say, *go get um, tiger,* as he turned to give her some privacy.

Rachel held her hand out, taking claim of the red satin prop.

Shayla's jaw clenched and her eyes crinkled, shooting daggers at Carrie Ann as she relinquished the heart. "You *so* owe me. Big time."

She gripped the board, lifted her chin, poked her bum out and trotted nude into the surf.

Rachel followed behind, heart in hand, thigh deep in the frigid November ocean.

Shayla bobbed up and down on the slow rolling breakers. *Five yards is far enough.* Her teeth chattered while Rachel applied a fresh coat of lip gloss and dried her hands on a towel she carried slung over her shoulder.

Adjusting her precarious position, Shayla sat tall on the surfboard. Her nipples constricted so tightly they ached from the cold water.

Tony stood on the beach fine-tuning his focus

through the zoom lens.

She took a quick sweeping glance downward, her goody box shone plain as day in the afternoon sun. "I'm feeling a little exposed here, Tony!"

"You look beautiful, sweetheart. That's perfect."

I bet! One more sweetheart out of you and I might just kick you in the shin! She took a deep, cleansing breath followed by another, casting out her modesty and the frosty chill of the cold water.

"You look hot, Shay!" Carrie Ann shouted her approval, fully clothed from the comfort of the warm sand. "Let's get the show on the road. We've got a gala to get ready for!"

Sunrays streamed down from the blue sky, heating the curve of her backside and the board beneath her bottom. The wide surfboard lifted her completely out of the water, giving her a very open visual perspective at herself. She felt sexy. Exhilarating pings of stimulation tingled her tummy and below. If it weren't for Tony watching from the beach, she could've embraced this moment. She'd always been comfortable with her body image, but in that precise moment, her vulnerability turned to empowerment. An invigorating feeling of freedom and excitement washed over her.

Her face flushed as desire and longing turned to frustration and irritation. All roads lead to home...she was horny.

Grabbing hold of the heart, she wedged it between her thighs and gripped her fingers over each hump. She cocked her head and gave Tony a sultry grin, knowing how her night would end.

Tony had captured the perfect photo within five minutes.

Shayla assumed the worst part of the day was over when she heard *That's a wrap!*, but she was wrong. Following a long, hot shower, she fell to another round of four different curling irons and nine separate makeup brushes, all of which Rachel assured were a necessity for every woman's bag of tricks. Sitting still long enough for one makeover was tolerable, but two in one day compared to a trip to the gynecologist *and* dentist, until she examined herself in the mirror.

All primped and in her stunning red dress, Shayla had never felt more glamorous in her life.

Carrie Ann entered the dressing closet, giving Shayla the once over.

Staring wide-eyed into the full-length mirror, she pinched at the shirring on the left side, positioning the jeweled pin at the cinch of her waist. The loosely pleated fabric draped down the natural waist of the sophisticated gown to the tip of her perfectly painted toes. Shayla loved to shop for everything *except* designer dresses. She'd never even attended her prom and Carrie Ann had always helped her choose dresses for every other red carpet event. She turned, proudly showing off the drape, which exposed her bronze back. "The sales lady said it's stylish, elegant and refined. What do you think?"

Carrie Ann lifted her shoulders and raised her brows raised in speculation.

"What?" she questioned apprehensively.

"You look..." Carrie Ann paused, circling her in a stalking fashion. "Fabulous. Rachel did an amazing job on your hair and makeup."

"I feel a *but* coming on."

"*But*, red is the color of the night. You don't want to be the shrinking violet. You need to be the bouquet of roses at full bloom."

"If I get any fuller, I might combust." Anticlimax drowned her tone.

"Exactly" Carrie Ann rummaged through the drawers, retrieving a pair of scissors. She knelt on the ground in front of Shayla, giving the sheers a quick *snip snip*.

"What the hell are you doing?" Shayla gasped, taking three steps back. "I spent a full week's pay on this dress!"

"It is lovely and classic *and* unfortunately boring as hell. It certainly doesn't say *come fuck me, Mat* at all! Do I need to remind you that you haven't gotten laid in a month?"

Shayla shook her head. "But tonight isn't about—"

Carrie Ann raised her pointer finger to Shayla's lips. She crept closer and grabbed hold of the hem of her dress. "It's simply missing the wow factor."

She ran the sheers up the side of her dress to the top of her thigh. The slit remained hidden behind the loose ruffle until she spread her legs hip width apart. "You can thank me later."

****

Shayla graced the stage with confidence and conviction. She spoke of the continuing efforts in the fight against heart disease and a call to action, inviting people to *Bare Their Souls* and share their stories. As she announced the Humanitarian Award, the ballroom erupted with applause honoring the outstanding individual, a world-renowned chef making a difference in food culture on a global scale.

Attendees rose from their seats, giving a standing ovation, but Mat's chair sitting center stage three tables back, remained blatantly vacant.

As Shayla exited the stage, Carrie Ann was waiting in the wings with a glass of Shayla's favorite poison, Kentucky whiskey.

"Sorry Shay, I know you really wanted him to be here."

"No, I understand. Mat's dedicated to his job and his family. No man or relationship is going to be perfect. He's very giving and devoted. Those are great qualities in a man." Her voice sounded dismal even to her own ears.

As the emcee called people to the floor, Carrie Ann wrinkled her nose with a pathetic scoff. "That's complete bullshit, but if it makes you feel better, keep telling yourself that. The man *is* devoted as long as it looks good in the public eye. You know I adore him, but calculated kindness runs in his genes. It doesn't matter if you are in his bed or wearing his ring on your finger, Mat is *married* to politics."

"I'm not completely sold on the possibility of wearing his ring." Shayla shirked coolly at the idea of marriage, then wriggled her brow with a sly grin. "But I am fascinated with his thread count."

"You have to be in his bed in order to count the threads, Shayla." Carrie Ann reminded, nodding toward the opposite end of the crowded room, observing Mat as he greeted California's elite. "He should've been here on time. And don't take any crap for helping me out today. By the way, I forgot to tell you, you're Miss July."

"July? What?" The word centerfold quickly added to her growing tension.

Mat approached Shayla, pressing a quick kiss to her cheek. "Sorry I'm late. Hello Carrie Ann. Congratulations, it looks like another successful year.

Grateful donors are opening up their hearts and their checkbooks for a great cause."

"Thanks, but save it. I'll leave the two of you alone." Carrie Ann patted him on the lapel of his jacket before walking away.

"I needed to close the deal, Shayla. After eighteen years in the Senate, my father's affair left a bad taste in the mouth for most Californians. It was an embarrassment to our family name. My mother has a chance to repair the Huntston image and do great things for this state."

Shayla listened to his eloquent well-rehearsed apology. She knew Mat was uncomfortable talking about his father's ramped affairs and the pain it caused still lingered in his voice. "Let's just forget about it and try to enjoy what's left of the night."

Clasping her petite fingers around her whiskey tumbler, she nursed the sweet smoky liquid and moseyed into the auction room.

Mat schmoozed the California elite while guiding her through the room. Uncertain if she truly accepted his excuses for the delay or if it was the sheer fact he was so damn compelling, she opted not to make a big deal of it. Yet the fact she'd fully expected the evening to play out exactly as it had nagged at her, causing her stomach to coil with tension.

Shayla spent an hour listening to him maneuver effortlessly through each conversation, treading gingerly over his campaign message, repeating the same lines to each new couple they approached. Strolling by an exquisite painting of an elderly grey-haired woman, Shayla recalled one of her grandma's favorite sayings. *That young man can talk the bark off a tree, but does he have deep roots?*

Perusing table by table, Shayla took mental notes of raffle items she considered bidding on. Several provoked her interest, each involved a fantastic travel package or an adrenaline filled getaway.

Famed pop star, La Mea stood beside her, sporting a leopard spandex dress with a cut out on the stomach, allowing her baby bump to make its debut appearance. "Maybe we should bid on the Vegas wedding."

Her baby-daddy, renowned rapper Biggie Tug, soothed his hand in a circle over the protruding belly and nestled into her heavily jeweled neck. "Maybe we should."

Tug reached for a pen and a bidding card as La Mea leaned in, placing a kiss of affection to his neck.

The tender moment pulled a heartfelt smile from Shayla and she dropped her view to the white cloth covering the table, not wanting to intrude.

La Mea handed her a pen and tossed Shayla a sweet smile. "What are you and your man bidding on, hun?"

"Me?" she answered in surprise. A deep notch of concentration settled in a groove between her brows. Standing motionless in front of a table with pen in hand, Shayla scanned over the gifts tapping the pen on the rim of her glass. "We haven't decided. I have no idea what he would really enjoy."

"He's a man, honey. It can't be too difficult." She gave a sultry wink, clutching to Biggie Tug's arm as they sauntered down the aisle.

Mat's good character, easy temperament and polarizing charm made up for the few flaws and deep-rooted differences between them. He loved an office; she loved the great outdoors. His idea of a great vacation included national monuments; hers included national top ten beaches. After more than a year of dating, Shayla took a calculating look around the room, unable to write their names on a single raffle items they could enjoy together. *What exactly do we have in common?*

Mat's swaying voice hummed in the background. The repetitive dialogue made her stomach flip and anxious perspiration gathered at the nape of her neck. Shrugging off the tension gathering around her thoughts, she laid the pen on the table.

Mat gently clasped the back of her elbow, exiting the room without even noticing she hadn't bid on anything.

By the end of the evening his lack in emotional intimacy made her wonder if their relationship would ever be enough. Enough to last a lifetime. Mat offered so many wonderful characteristics, but she questioned if they were truly compatible. Two months ago, after an argument, she wrote a list of Mat's good and not so good traits, expecting the answer to be plain. Clearly, just like everything else in her life, nothing was black and white. They were cut from different cloth; she from a hand-me-down pair of jeans and Mat from the finest spun silk. In the beginning, their differences brought balance to their relationship, but now it felt more as if they lacked a deep connection.

Shayla sat quietly, immersed in the darkness of the car ride home.

He hadn't given her a good job or a customary congratulations. He hadn't even told her she looked beautiful. The entire evening revolved around gathering votes. Her agitation escalated as Mat's trivial chatter permeated the stillness of her mind. It'd been so long since they'd made love. She intended for the evening to end in intimate celebration. The more he rattled on, however, the more she focused on his seeming incapability of acknowledging her.

Nothing felt intimate.

Arriving at his plush house in the hills, they followed routine.

Mat tossed his keys on the bedside table, took off his jacket and poured a drink. Shayla traipsed into the bathroom to undress. Hanging her gown on the back of the door, she released a heavy sigh, staring at her overnight bag on the tile floor. Fumbling with zipper, she opened the bag and pulled out a sexy negligee she'd purchased. *Nothing seems special or romantic tonight.*

Plucking her gloss from the bag, she gazed into the mirror, methodically dabbing it to her lips. She tried to pin her irritation and hostility to the one thing upsetting her, but it was a million little things. *Maybe I'm just PMSing.* She huffed, convincing herself she was being silly.

Opening the door, she inhaled deeply, exhaling out a soft chuckle. *Maybe I simply have pent up frustrations.*

She moseyed around the foot of the bed, the side of the bed where he sat still fully clothed. He swept an assessing gaze down her body, offering an approving smile of her sheer baby blue nighty. Reaching for her hand, Mat nodded. "Yes, Cecil promises his support."

Her vision turned fuzzy. Her chest fell heavy with insult as she realized he was on the phone. Shayla yanked her hand free. Crossing her arms over her chest, she paced back and forth at the end of the bed. Uncontrollable tears blurring her vision, she wiped the wetness from her cheeks.

"He has several new ideas on polling strate-
gies and promised to schedule some meetings in
Washington."

Sinking in dejection, Shayla drowned out his
endless pats on the back as the minutes ticked by.
She didn't even bother acknowledging him when he
said, "I just need to make one more phone call."

Her eyes remained fixed on the floor as she
grinded her toes into the design of the plush Berber
carpet.

Anger, confusion and rejection rippled down
her spine, leaving her heart and self esteem in sham-
bles. After what seemed like thirty minutes, she retreated into his closet. Shayla stripped off her nighty,
casting it to the floor. Searching numbly through a
drawer of her belongings, she yanked on a pair of
jeans and sweatshirt.

She marched barefoot into the room and
snatched his car keys from the bedside table, her
gown draped across her arm and heels dangling
from her fingertips.

Mat held the phone to his chest, muffling his
conversation in his turtleneck sweater. He stood from
the bed, surprise blanching over his face as if he
couldn't believe his eyes. "Where are you going?"

"Home."

"What?" He gaped at her incredulously before responding to the caller. "I'll have to call you
back in the morning."

"Don't bother. I can't do this. I'm leaving."

He closed the phone and reached for her arm.
"Stop being silly. You don't know what you're saying."

She angled her head, staring at his grasp. Her

heartbeat turned unruly hearing Mat repeat the shrilling words her father used to say to her mother after a long night of drunken fighting. Memories came in waves, sending tsunami-warning bells crushing over her. *This isn't right*, came a small protective voice.

He released her arm, raising both hands in the air. "Shayla, come on, don't be ridiculous. It's simply—"

"It's business. I know." His lack of emotional intimacy and incapability to acknowledge her feelings eddied, sending her hurt emotions slamming to the ocean floor. She made her way toward the door leading to the garage, hiding the slick of hot tears streaming down her cheeks.

"You acting like—"

She closed the door on him, locking out his words of rebuke. Treating her as a child was a huge flaw, like pouring whiskey on a fire. Shayla didn't have a clear vision of where their relationship was going, but she headed home alone.

CHAPTER THREE

Sounds of Sunday morning resonated through the window cracked open. Shayla lay half awake, listening to the rumble of lawn mowers and traffic heading toward the beach.

Ring.

She rolled on her back, pulling the down pillow over her head.

Ring.

Shayla exhaled with a loud groan, slapping both arms flat against the mattress, not wanting to start the day. It was too early for Carrie Ann to call, which meant it'd be Mat and she wasn't ready to talk to him yet.

Ring.

"Shit!" she snarled with an eye roll. Hiding under her pillow wouldn't help or make him go away. "He barely acknowledges me for weeks and *now* he wants to fix it!"

"Hello," she answered curtly.

"Good morning." Her uncle's deep voice on the other end of the line brought a smile of relief.

Chucking the pillow aside, she sat up in bed cross-legged. "Good morning."

"Are you sure? That didn't sound like a good morning." Playful humor filtered in his tone. "You're not hung over from last night, are you?"

"No." A grin tugged at the corner of her mouth. She never drank enough to get hung over. "Believe it or not I'm still laying in bed."

"The weather's so nice, I figured you might've snuck out of his place and hit your board early this morning."

"Oh, I...I stayed at my place last night." She hesitated slightly. Though her uncle never said anything horrible about Mat, he wasn't a big fan. "Are you in town?"

Shayla didn't expect to see her Uncle for another week. She was flying to Colorado then to spend Thanksgiving with him and his new girlfriend and her kids.

"Not yet. We'll be there this afternoon. Can you get the place ready for us? I know it's not much notice. I've got that birthday party to go to."

"Do I have your schedule marked wrong? I didn't think you were attending the party, so I sent a card along with a bottle of brandy and fifty of his favorite caramel apples." Uncle Tommy was known for practical jokes and his long time friend and producer, Larry Hart, was turning fifty.

"That explains why my phone's been ringing off the hook with some colorful threats. Apparently, I will be disavowed if I don't make an appearance," he ribbed. "I'd love to introduce Tess to Larry too. We'll only be in town a few days, so I just need you to stock the fridge. Oh, and turn the pool heat on. She loves to swim."

"Of course." She cleared throat with a subtle chortle at his usage of we, us and she. Her uncle *never* used the word *love* when it came to a woman, let alone twice in one paragraph. "I'm sure Tess will *love* that."

Being a personal assistant to a famous Holly-wood heartthrob, Shayla discovered early on to ig-nore harsh judgments made by the public who re-ceived their information from photographers who hunted and exploited celebrities. Women swooned over her uncle and went to great lengths to get their picture taken with him, not to mention items they sent in the mail. Little did they know, all of their un-dergarments went straight into the trash. His new girlfriend, Tess, seemed different from other women he dated for a host of reasons. She wasn't an actress or famous, she was his age and had several grown children, and Tess also carried a genuine aura of warmth and kindness.

"If I don't get the chance to see you, be sure to email me your flight information for Thanksgiving."

"Will do. And have fun. For the record, I real-ly like her."

He gave a husky laugh of appreciation. "Me too, Shay. Me too."

Tossing the phone aside, she climbed out of the comfort of her warm bed and stretched, raising her hands to the ceiling. Bending at the waist, she placed her palms on the floor with a groan.

Ring.

She flopped back onto the bed, searching through the piles of fluffy white down comforter. Grasping the phone on the fifth ring, she answered, "What'd you forget?"

"That's the answer I was hoping to hear." Mat's tone dripped with apology. "Good morning."

Her lips pursed tight. Dread welled in her throat. "Hey."

"I'm out front. Can I come in?"

"Yeah." She subconsciously raked her fingers through the leftover curls in her hair. Scooting off the bed, she tugged a tank top over her head. "Just come around back."

Plodding into the kitchen, she unlocked the door and lit the burner beneath the stainless steel teakettle. Leaning her hip against the counter, she folded her arms across her chest, bracing for another long discussion. Mat didn't argue. He preferred to deliberate, and he was good at it.

He walked in wearing a rueful smile, dressed for work in black slacks, a button down shirt and a white to-go cup in each hand. Mat offered her a cup of tea and leaned against the counter beside her, scrutinizing her mood. "I'm sorry."

She unconsciously scratched at her upper arm allowing time to pass.

He tilted his head, leaning lower to capture her attention. "I'm sorry, Shayla."

She peered into his blue eyes for a moment. Doubt carved it's way into her heart. "I just don't think—"

"Spend the weekend with me."

Her insides twisted with uncertainty. "I don't know, Mat."

"I was a jerk last night. Let me make it up to you." A wisp of desperation clung to his promise. "Stay home and spend Thanksgiving with me and my family."

Sensing the weighted worry in his voice, she let her gaze drift out the window to the ocean, hoping to calm the inner turmoil etching up her throat. "I'm supposed to be going to Colorado. You know that."

He pulled her into his chest, clumsily patting

her back.

She startled at the unusual show of affection.

"I won't work. It will be the best Thanksgiving, unlike anything you've ever had."

Her heart pounded as he danced gingerly around old wounds from her past. She'd quit looking back years ago on painful holiday memories with her mother and father. Peering out at the waves in the distance, she was uncertain if he'd use her poignant childhood memories to manipulate her decision or if his offer was sincere. She dabbed her fingertip to the corner of her eye.

"Please? Let me make it up to you."

The idea of spending a traditional holiday as a family had only been a dream. Unfortunately, she grew up experiencing the nightmare of her parents. Fraught with broken emotion, she nodded with a sniffle. "Okay."

****

Carrie Ann roared with laughter. "You're spending the *entire* day there?"

"Yes, so I need help deciding what to wear." Shayla cluelessly stared at thirty dresses hanging in her closet. This was the first time she'd attend a formal family gathering at Mat's family estate. "And what should I take?"

"Whiskey! You'll need a fifth of whisky to survive, Shay."

"Huh?" Anxiety turned to alarm as she tucked the phone between her ear and shoulder, flipping through her wardrobe. "It can't be that bad."

"Shayla that woman is fierce! Mrs. Huntston is a card-carrying member of the bitch club! With a capital B! If you're expecting this to be a sweet wholesome Betty-fucking-Crocker gathering, you'd better think again."

"Mat said—"

"Mat said what? Shayla, whose opinion are you going to trust? Mine or his?" Carrie Ann didn't bother waiting for a response. "Mat isn't going to warn you. Hell, he probably thinks you will fit right in. He wears blinders when it comes to his family. That woman preys on his sense of loyalty, and no offense, but Mat doesn't have the biggest spine. He's been groomed for years to be the Huntston succession to the political throne. How do you think she got him to take the leadership role of her campaign?"

"But—"

"Trust me on this, Shayla. By the end of the day you'll need a drink."

Taking Carrie Ann's advice, Shayla arrived bearing a high-end bottle of whisky. Mrs. Huntston received them in the grand foyer with a formal greeting. "Hello, Mathew. You know how much I dislike it when you're late."

"Happy Thanksgiving, Mother. My apologies. Shayla needed a few extra minutes."

Standing frozen beneath the lavish chandelier, Shayla gripped to the bottle of society whisky for moral support, obviously she wasn't going to get it from Mat who'd just thrown her under the bus.

"I'm glad you could join my family for Thanksgiving, Shayla." Pleasant distain seeped from her voice.

"Thank you for having me."

Mrs. Huntston wore a smile, but Shayla feared piranha teeth hid behind her perfectly applied lipstick, masking the color of her true emotions. Shayla offered the fine amber liquid to Mat's mother, however she declined.

"I don't drink whiskey. You can leave it in the kitchen with—"

"Hello dear. I'll take that. Come join me, will you?" An impeccably dressed elderly woman snatched the bottle from her hands.

"Shayla, this is my grandmother, Alice."

"Finally, someone with good taste." Alice inspected the bottle with appreciation. She crooked her finger, gesturing Shayla to follow. "Come with me dear. I'll get some glasses."

Shayla politely declined the first offer to join her in a tottie, but after an hour of introductions to Mat's stately extended family, she gladly accepted hoping to calm her nerves. Every interaction with his mother felt daunting.

Over the last ten years, Shayla had spent a significant amount of time around people with means, but the Huntston family was an entirely new breed of wealth. Everything about *The Estate* reeked of grandeur. Opulent historical furnishings filled the home. Merely sitting on the extravagant antique sofa became a chore. The cream and gold toned paisley textile felt more like a tapestry than fabric.

She began analyzing her every movement. *Do I sit back? Should I cross my legs traditionally or at the ankles? Should I set my crystal glass on the cherry wood coffee table?* She opted to sit forward, cross at the ankles and cling to her glass.

If the simple act of sitting on the sofa wasn't enough strain on her brain, she had to endure formal introductions and affluent conversations driven around politics.

Mat remained by her side, guiding her through greetings and discussions. However, he also repeated and reworded her sentences several times so she sounded scholarly and more acceptable to his vastly cultured family.

Mat pushed her too far when his brother asked, "Shayla would you care for an hors d'oeuvre?"

Shayla replied, "Sure, thanks."

Mat corrected her, saying, "Yes, thank you."

She openly cringed, ignoring the correction defiantly.

By the time chef announced dinner was served, Shayla's nerves were so frazzled, panic swelled at the mere thought of silverware and china place settings.

Mrs. Huntston graced the head of the Victorian table lined with twenty-four chairs. Mat sat on one side her, his younger brother on the other. She stood. "We all have so much to be thankful for. Let's each take the time to share what wonderful blessings have occurred in our lives this year."

Good old-fashioned fun left the building, and present day anxiety landed in her lap. Shayla gripped Mat's thigh beneath the table, digging her nails into him. "You should've warned me about this."

"Mathew, let's start with you." Mrs. Huntston gave a slow measured nod toward her oldest son. Scrutinizing Shayla's distress, she proposed in a cold and steady tone, "Or would you prefer for your brother to begin?"

"Thank you. Actually, I would prefer to go first." Mat patted her hand, releasing her death grip from his thigh. He scooted his chair away from the table. Placing his palm to his chest, he bowed slightly toward his mother. "This year marks a new beginning for the Huntston family, that of which I am born into," — he turned toward Shalya, scooping up her hand in his — "and that of which I hope to begin."

Anxiety warbled her complete attention. She'd heard a varied version of this speech so many times. She smiled politely, somewhat tuning out his monotone language, until he bent and dropped to one knee.

"Shayla Clemmins — "

"What are you doing?" Her breathing instantly turned fast and shallow. Shayla's eyes darted cagily around the table and back to Mat before dropping to an open box revealing an engagement ring.

"Shayla," he repeated, drawing her focus to his face.

Over his shoulder, she caught a glimpse of his mother's furious face turning ashen white before her eyes. Overcome with the sudden urge to run, she squirmed in her seat.

Mat squeezed her fingers and smiled joyfully into her eyes. "Will you marry me?"

Time stood still.

Air trapped in her lungs.

Finally, she released a long deep exhale.

"Mat," she whispered with one tiny shake of her head, barely enough for anyone else to notice.

Grandma Alice snarked with a hiccup, "Married? I always thought that boy was gay."

"Mother!" Mrs. Huntston barked with a snap of her fingers.

"I thought — " Mat suddenly lost his power of speech.

"I'm just so…surprised." Shame tangled with the words, strangling her throat. She didn't want to hurt him, but their relationship had been riddled with uncertainty lately. She laid her hand on his forearm and he tensed beneath her touch. "I just need some time to think about it. That's all."

The room fell silent, hanging on the edge of awkward impatience.

She watched as his poignant, humiliated gaze swept around the table. Shayla fought the urge to bolt under the watchful stares of his family and shocking gasps adding to her increasing discomfort. If looks could kill, Shayla would be road kill. She shivered as fear coiled in the pit of her stomach.

"Of course." Mat rose to his feet in a state of confusion. "Excuse me."

Silently, Shayla followed, rushing down the hall to a library. Heartbreaking tears rolled down her face and dripped off her jaw, falling to the marble floor.

He closed the door partially behind them.

"I don't know what to say," she answered sincerely, burying her face in her hands. "I'm not saying no. It's just..."

She turned toward him, wanting to hold and comfort him, but he sat rigid half on the edge of a desk with his arms folded and fists stuffed under his arms.

"Well you are sure as hell not saying yes either." A new angry edge clung to his tone. He took a ragged breath.

Blood pounded in her temples. She went to him, tucking her fingers in the folds of his arms. "You caught me off guard and...and we've been arguing a lot. I never get to see you."

"I know I screwed up at the gala. I want to prove to you that you mean more than anything to me. I thought—"

A knock sounded at the door.

Mrs. Huntston marched across the threshold. Her blade thin lips stretched tight and anger darted from her stare. She stood chest to chest with Mat, throwing her finger in his face. "What the hell are you doing?"

"Mother, this is—"

"And you!" She turned, lurching toward Shayla, animosity humming between them. "Who do you think you are? How dare you embarrass me like that? As if posing *nude* wasn't bad enough! Now you have the audacity to say *I just need time to think about it!*"

A flicker of shame crawled over her flesh. "I'm just being honest."

"Now you decide to have morals?"

"I apologize if I embarrassed either one of you, but I need to be certain." Gaining her wits, Shayla raised her chin indignantly. Her arms fell stiff at her side holding her hands in tight fists. "And I have morals. I posed nude to raise money and much needed awareness to heart disease."

"You took your clothes off for the entire world to see. Did you bother to consider for one second the backlash your attention-whore antics cost me?" A vein near Mrs. Huntston's left eye bulged as her face turned red.

Anger splintered and flashed like a warning beacon. "You have no right to judge me, Mrs. Huntston. None."

Mat interceded. "Shayla, can you give my mother and I a few minutes?"

"Gladly."

Raised voices spilled into the hallway as she searched for a bathroom to retreat. Her hands trembled as she turned on the faucet. She splashed cool water on her face, washing away streaks of dark mascara. Her head was a mess and she needed time, time to think. Her hands lay flat on the counter as she stared at her reflection in the mirror. *What was he thinking?* Snatching a tissue from the box, she blew her nose and tossed it into the toilet before closing the lid and sitting on it. *You can't fix everything with a gift, Mat. That is much more than a bracelet or pair of earrings.*

Staring up at the ceiling, she dragged her fingertips unconsciously over her neck. She would never hurt him, but she couldn't give Mat the answer he was looking for, not yet anyway. When Mat asked her out on their first date, she felt like the luckiest girl in the world thinking, *How could a man like Mat Huntston be remotely interested in dating a girl like me?* Their backgrounds couldn't be any more contradictory, but at this point...

After a brief mental struggle of guilt verses rationality, she returned to the library.

Angry whispers escalated loud enough for her hear from behind the door. "It takes more than a beautiful girl in a bikini strapped to a surfboard to marry into *this* family, Mathew! You are a Huntston. Stop thinking with your penis. You're acting just like your father."

Mat said nothing, but Shayla envisioned the anger and hurt plastered to his face.

"We are making history. Is that what you want to contribute to your lineage? Your family heritage? The daughter of a drunk...an abuser? You're willing to dirty up our good name, leaving smudge marks on your future children?"

"I'm pretty sure my father already dirtied up our good name."

"She grew up in single wide trailer for Christ's sake." Mrs. Huntston paused. "We discussed this. I thought you were going to gain my campaign some Hollywood heavy hitters. Not get engaged to the niece of one it's biggest playboys!"

"With any luck you'll get both. I told you, I'll have his niece and his vote."

Every morsel of Shayla's trust crumbled like a sandcastle with the incoming tide as she lurked outside the door.

"I love her, Mother."

"You do what you have to do, but don't you dare fuck up my campaign."

The door opened and Mrs. Huntston glared at her with nark narrow eyes, not uttering a word.

A hot wave of resentment and rage replaced her shame and mortification. As if the proposal wasn't a big enough shock for her to consider, now she had to decide if Mat had dated her for the perks of campaign contribution or because he loved her.

Shayla entered the room, leaning her shoulder against the door jam. Her heart and cheeks burned with her rising fury. "Now I'm a vote? Or more importantly, should I say, my uncle's vote? How could you?"

Mat hung his head, scrubbing his hands over his face. "No, Shayla. You are not a vote and this has nothing to do with Tommy. That's my mother talking, not me."

"She said enough for both of you." The dark walls of the library felt like a cage. "I gotta get out of here. Take me home."

They didn't offer goodbyes or Happy Thanksgivings, simply walked out the door. After a brief silence, Mat apologized repeatedly for the searing words of his mother, swearing that had never been his intent.

Mat gazed out the windshield. "I won't lie, Shayla. I did calculate it'd be a win-win situation, you, the wedding and the campaign. It just seemed like the perfect solution."

Numbness from reality swirled around her kept her speechless for most of the drive. The forty-minute car ride felt like four hours. Judging by the pain and anguish in his eyes, she believed him. His mind worked analytically and she didn't doubt his intention aimed for a perfect solution. Unfortunately, there would be no easy systematic answer for what just happened. Being a mere piece of the puzzle would never be enough.

Pulling into the driveway, he reached for her hand with an imploring and hopeful half-smile. "I want to fix this. Can I come in?"

"You can't fix every mistake with a gift, Mat. I need some space. I need to think."

"I'll give you the space you need, but I want you to wear this." He retrieved the brilliant engagement ring from his jacket pocket.

She shook her head, rejecting the offer, but he slipped it on her right hand instead of the left, making certain she had a symbolic, tangible token of his affection. "I do love you, Shayla. I thought—"

"It's not that I don't love you, Mat. I just need to take a break for a while and decide what the right choice is for me."

"Take the time you need, Shayla."

Mat was a *good* man and he'd make a good husband, but Shayla couldn't help but think he might not be the one for her.

CHAPTER FOUR

Winter arrived the day after Thanksgiving, dampening her spirits further. Refusing to submit to the dreary cold weather, she managed to get a few good swells in along with a handful of the regular board junkies on the beach.

After an anxiety-filled phone call full of confessions, Carrie Ann rushed over.

"I don't know if I want to marry Mat." Shayla shed no tears, but a deep frown remained tattooed to her forehead. "And his family...I don't fit in, especially now. His mother is so conniving. His proposal quickly turned into an all-about-her agenda. You should've seen the hatred in her eyes when I couldn't answer. And she slammed me for posing nude. She was livid."

"That woman is never going to accept you. If you say yes and marry him then she will *deal* with you, but she is never going to *like* you. It has nothing to do with you. That's her flaw, Shay. Not yours. And believe me, that bitch would approve if you posed naked for the benefit of her campaign."

"He's perfect in so many ways. He's smart, responsible, rational, generous—"

"Those are all great qualities, but how about what he doesn't give you? Sometimes the traits a man is missing can be just as crucial as the qualities he holds." They sat cross-legged at each end of the couch facing each other. Carrie Ann leaned forward, patting Shayla's knee, their bond more like sisters than best friends. "The fact you don't have an answer might be answer enough."

****

She dabbed concealer on the dark smudges of exhaustion lay beneath her eyes. Expelling a long exhale, she tossed the stick of cover-up back into her makeup bag. "It's no use."

She scoffed to the worn out reflection staring back in the mirror. "Nothing is going to cover these bags."

Shayla hadn't slept but hardly a few hours a night for the past week, and lack of sleep started to take its toll. She hadn't spoken to Mat in days. While he was being kind enough to give her the space she needed, their separation left Shayla no closer to an answer.

Her cell phone resting on the granite countertop buzzed, vibrating its way across the counter. Seeing her uncle's face scroll over the screen, she gave a tired smile, answering the phone. "You must be reading my mind. I've been thinking about you all morning and was going to call you."

Her voice sounded dismal even to her own ears. He knew her better than anyone else did. She desperately needed advice and Tommy would always give it to her straight. His warm laughter sparked a much needed smile of relief.

"You were?" He paused briefly, curiosity building in his tone. "What's going on, Shay? Everything okay?"

Tears and the week's events spilled out. At

one point she paused, her gaze anchored to the floor wondering if she should mention Mrs. Huntston's ulterior motives. Ultimately, she opted to keep Mat's mother's scheming intentions to herself. Her uncle was a force to be reckoned and very protective of her. He could bury Margaret and her campaign before it even got off the ground.

She knew what his answer would be, but couldn't resist asking through broken sniffles, "What do you think I should do?"

"Obviously, I don't believe in rushing into marriage. Only you can decide if Mat is the right guy for you. I'm proud of you for not caving under the pressure of his family." His tone turned pleasant and teasing. "As a matter of fact, it just so happens I have the perfect solution for you."

"You do?" She kidded back through a shaky breath.

"Yep. Pack your bags, Shayla. You're coming to Greece."

"Greece? I'm not coming to Greece." Water works threatened again as big tears blurred her vision. She was touched by his thoughtful offer. He would stop at nothing to cheer her up. "I'm not crashing your vacation with Tess."

"I'm not asking you." Her uncle cleared his throat, holding back his own emotions. "I'm getting married in four days. You're coming to Greece."

Speechless, she damn near dropped the phone.

"What?" Her jaw dropped open as she waited for the punch line. Full of excitement, she leapt to her feet and threw her hands in the air. "Shut the front door!"

"I'm doing it, Shay. I have finally found the

right woman."

"Oh, my God!" Heat radiated from her smile beaming from ear to ear. "I knew you loved her. I'm so happy you!"

"I'm not sure if a wedding is the perfect solution for your dilemma, but regardless—"

"Stop right there. I could not be happier, Unc. I wouldn't miss your wedding for anything."

"That's the good news. The bad news is that you are going to be very busy when I break the story. I want to handle this with kit gloves and control the announcement very sensitively. The blow back will be tremendous and Tess has no idea of what to expect."

"Got it. I'll take care of it. What can I do?" Her enthusiasm began to build. "Do you need me to get a hold of anyone? Flowers? Church? What do you need?"

"I've got most of it handled, but I need you to stop in Las Vegas on your way."

****

Taxiing into the Las Vegas terminal, Shayla unlatched her seatbelt and swallowed her pride. When Tommy asked her to make flight arrangements for Tess's three children, she politely agreed to schedule them a private jet further explaining she would depart from Los Angeles and meet them in Greece. Her uncle scoffed at the idea, insisting they fly together. Not wanting to sound like an angry toddler, she settled without ushering a word of complaint.

Shayla dressed casual in her favorite dark jeans and long-sleeved cotton sweater tee for the long flight. Her fingernails strummed against the fine leather armrest. She couldn't evade meeting Tess's kids forever. Unfortunately two of Tess's kids, Tracy and John, hadn't been welcoming to her uncle over the summer when he and Tess began dating. Her son's actions, attacking her uncle, verged on deplorable in Shayla's eyes. Even though Tommy assured her she'd love them, she remained skeptical.

Tommy was known for his list of girlfriends as much as he was for award winning movies. Granted, even though his reputation as a playboy was well deserved, she still resented the harsh judgment laid out by others. The media had a way of trivializing the good charity work he did, always accentuating his personal flaws.

Pressing the heel of her boot into the carpet, she obstinately scooted her bum deeper into the fine leather, allowing her head to fall against the headrest as the flight attendant opened the door.

Keeping her eyes closed wouldn't make them disappear.

Shayla lifted a lid. Peering toward the front of the cabin, she recognized Tess's oldest daughter by her long, dark, coppery hair. Tommy described her as a younger version of Tess with a reserved personality.

"Hi." Tracy's mane fell over one shoulder as she extended her hand to the flight attendant. Catching Shayla out of the corner of her eye, she nodded with a small smile, taking in the surroundings of the private jet. "Wow."

Rising out of her seat, Shayla took a deep breath, attempting to shake off her preconceived grudge. After all, they were about to become family.

"You must be Tracy." Shayla held out her hand, only to be greeted with an exuberant smile and warm embrace.

"I am."

Tracy's casual sexy smile mimicked her mother's. The cast of red in her hair accentuated her blue eyes and the term pin-up girl suited her perfectly. Her gracious figure filled out her skinny jeans and tan blazer to perfection, giving her a sensible chic vibe.

Her younger sister trotted up the steps and burst through the door bringing in the radiant sunshine right along with her wide smile. She gave a quick wave to the attendant and tossed her designer bag on the closest seat. "Holy shit!"

"Hello." Shayla choked out a subtle laugh, surprised by their good-natured amiability.

Flying on a private jet had the tendency of making a great impression. She typically flew first class, at her uncle's insistence when she traveled for work. Shayla had flown on a private jet several times over the years, but it always felt like the first time. It gave the illusion of checking in to a posh resort, leaving her with the urge to inspect the luxurious bathroom amenities and expensive chocolate placed on a dish beside her bed.

"This is my little sister, JC."

JC danced down the aisle with a lively swagger, casting her arms wide, circling around Shayla and Tracy. JC towered over each of them by a foot with heels on. "Damn!" she squealed gleefully. "This is off the hook!"

Their radiant smiles and charismatic energy were instantly contagious, easing Shayla's reservations.

JC pranced down the aisle, taking in the luxurious amenities of the jet. Her caramel hair, pulled back tight in a stylish ponytail, bounced up and down with her enthusiasm. She nodded in approval plopping down into her seat. "Now this is the way to fly."

"Don't let her fool you, she hates to fly." Tess's son's full robust voice filled the cabin, sending chills down her arms. His eyes made a lazy descent down her body and returned to her face. He ambled carelessly into the cabin, wide shoulders nearly filling the passageway.

Dropping her smile, Shayla took aim, shooting him an icy glare. He was unapologetically masculine at a solid six-foot-two, physically fit and ready to take on anyone who got in his way. A muscle jumped in her jaw as a wave of fury washed over her comparing the size difference between him and her uncle. *Tommy would never stand a chance against those guns.*

His powerful build and an over arrogant attitude could have been construed by some as confidence, but Shayla viewed him as a bar room bully. She vowed a long time ago never to be intimidated by a man like him again. A lifetime of her father was enough.

He started toward her with measured strides. She blatantly turned her back, directing her full attention to the attendant. Heat skittered up her spine, spreading over her skin as she remained fully aware of a large male presence lingering directly behind her. After a brief conversation regarding scheduling and meal planning, Shayla turned to take her seat nearly bumping face first into his solid chest. Disregarding his faint smile tucked into the corner of his wide mouth, she attempted to go around him.

He shifted directly in front of her, extending his hand, "Hi, I'm John."

Her gaze flickered at the coffee colored Henley stretching over his flexing bicep. Her lip curled as a warning for him to get out of her way. "Shayla," she announced curtly, dodging his gesture of a friendly *hello* and settling into her seat with a *humff.*

Judging by the astonished look on his face, John seemed stunned by her snub. He raked his fingers through the short layers of his dark hair and glanced around the lavish interior, blinking repeatedly as if replaying what just happened. His glower molded into a grin, forming a wrinkle on his sun-chapped complexion.

Arrogant smiles were a dime a dozen in LA, but his egotistical grin sent blood surging through her veins, turning her cheeks crimson. His condescending smirk only deepened her urge to yell at him. He was such an unredeemable jerk. She wanted to stomp on his toe or, with a bit of encouragement, kick him in the chin.

The attendant methodically inspected the cabin, advising everyone to take their seats and prepare for takeoff.

John motioned for Shayla to scoot over so he could sit beside her.

"No," she snarled, appalled at the request, pointing at several other vacant seats.

Tracy and JC settled into individual recliners a row ahead of her. Tracy recited words of encouragement in a monotone voice, coaching her sister through take off.

Rays of sunlight cast through the window, igniting interest in his eyes. She froze, momentarily arrested by his intense gaze.

John placed a palm on the headrest, easing his ripped chest closer to her face, giving her no other choice but to move over and allow him to sit beside her. Sliding across the leather, Shayla allowed her gaze to drift down his jean denim clad hips lowering to take his seat.

Shayla grimaced, silently huddling next to the window, huffily crossing one leg over the other and both arms across her chest.

"How long is the flight, Shayla?" He pronounced her name mockingly, provoking Shayla's anger.

She lowered the armrest between them and narrowed her eyes in a glare of resentment. "Fourteen hours, *John*." Unable to stop herself, she continued with her own jab. "Or should I call you, *Rocky*?"

Offhanded amusement wandered across his lips. "Is that what this is about?"

"How about *Muhammad Ali* or *Sugar Ray*?"

Their gazes battled for a long moment.

John's haughty grin widened at her irritancy. "Tom got off pretty lucky...considering." His voice was thick with insinuation.

"Considering!" She gasped, unable to hold back an unnerving glare. "My uncle didn't do anything to you and you...you *attacked* him!"

John twisted, leaning on the armrest to get closer. "I had plenty of reasons to kick his ass." His lips pulled back full, exposing a sexy white smile that would've made most women eagerly line up at the sperm bank. "I thought he cheated on my mother."

"You beat him up for no reason." Her heartbeat slammed against her chest and dampness gathered at the nape of her neck.

He scoffed with a long, graceful shrug of his muscular shoulder. "I didn't beat him up. I just punched him a few times."

"You gave him two huge black eyes!" She fumed. Shayla, who'd never in her life laid a hand on anyone, reached out and poked him in the chest. "You're lucky you didn't break his nose. Do you have any idea how horrible that would've been? Do you? He makes his living off his face!"

John glanced comically at the crinkle in his shirt left by the imprint of her finger. He moved closer, inches from her face. "Lucky for him it was a misunderstanding. If he really had cheated on my mother," — he backed away with an arrogant grin — "well…"

"Well, what?" Shayla swallowed hard, peering into the most gorgeous emerald eyes looming near the shade of vibrant moss.

"Well let's just say he'd probably require plastic surgery." A smirk curled at the edge of his mouth as he took in every nuance of her angered face. Each muscle on her face strung tight with revulsion. His smile broadened. John rested his large palm on her forearm, "Calm down, I'm only messing with you a bit."

Annoyed, she squirmed free of his touch, the tenderness of it tingling all the way to her toes. Staring at his chiseled face, Shayla felt her rigid composure chipping away.

Untailored charm caressed every inch of his long athletic physique. His grin softened at her silence, causing her chest to feel tight and warm. A small horizontal scar above his left cheek captured her attention. She wondered who in their right mind would be tough enough to go toe-to-toe with this man.

"Tom and I are fine." He shrugged nonchalantly. "I like him, and better yet, my mother is crazy about him. That's what's important." He paused. "As long as he doesn't hurt her."

Her lip snarled at his warning, but her concern quickly shifted hearing the words doggie bag coming from the seats in front of them. Tracy asked the attendant for a short list of items, cool rag, clear soda and a few crackers.

"Is she gonna be all right?"

"JC has a severe fear of flying. Take off is the worst part. She'll be okay after we get in the air." Worry pinched his forehead. Powerful muscles shaped his long legs as he inched forward, straddling JC's seat from behind. Tucking his arms around the chair from both sides, he massaged her shoulders.

JC released a long shaky sigh.

"It's okay, sis, just relax. Close your eyes and take a deep breath," he said softly.

She watched silently as JC grasped his hand, holding on to it for dear life. Shayla unbuckled and wriggled forward to get a better view. JC's head tilted back and the pink blush dusting her cheeks moments ago turned ashen white under the overhead lights. Her eyes remained closed while she concentrated on deep breathing through pursed lips.

"She seemed fine when she got on the plane," Shayla stated in a hushed voice.

He continued rubbing, keeping physical contact with JC. "She tries to psych herself out before she flies. Especially today. It's such a long flight and she wanted to enjoy her first private jet experience. She's been *willing* a happy flight for two days."

"Manifesting, John. I've been manifesting a great flight." JC grumbled with heavy breath, peeking through the seats. "I'm subconsciously making it happen."

John mouthed quietly. "She reads one book and now she can control the outcome of her life."

JC scowled, turning to point a finger at her brother. "I heard that. Manifesting is the art of creating what you want at the time you want it. Don't make fun of me."

Shayla smiled, happy to see JC's color returning with her feistiness. "It's kind of like mind over matter."

"Not you too?" John frowned.

Every preconceived notion of John as a tough guy or an intimidating bully began to fade like the ground beneath the plane as they took off higher into the sky. John treated his sister with the compassion of a loving brother or a small child taking care of an injured animal.

John's elbow came to rest on Shayla's knee as they gathered at the crack between the seats. The dusting of dark hair on his brawny arm stood at attention. She startled at the sight of his goose bumps. He ran a slow burning gaze over her legs. The flight attendant broke his stare as she handed out fluffy pillows and down blankets.

After days with a lack of sleep, Shayla let out a big yawn. Merely catching sight of a pillow made her drowsy. Preparing for the long flight, she kicked off her boots and tucked her legs up under her bum, snuggling into her chair. The combined stress of Thanksgiving, Mat's proposal and her angst about meeting the man sitting beside her had taken its toll. Shayla tucked the white throw under her chin, adjusting the soft pillow beneath her head.

JC had calmed down considerably, and the girls all settled in for the long flight ahead. Tracy turned on a movie and they burrowed into their recliners.

"Are all of you going to sleep?" His disappointment echoed through the plane.

His sisters each raised a hand in the air. "Yep. Night, Romeo. See you in Greece."

"Greece? That's at least twelve hours away!" His gaze wandered over Shayla. "Are you going to sleep too?"

She yawned again. "I've had a really long, rough week. They have a great selection of movies."

Thankful for the opportunity to give in to her collapse, her lids closed and she took a deep, cleansing breath. The scent of John's cologne sparked her senses. Glinting through tired slits, she noticed he examined the ring on her finger with a puzzled frown. Shayla tucked her hands tighter into the folds of down.

"No hard feelings?" He held out his hand again.

A flirt of a smile tugged at her mouth. "I wouldn't count on it."

CHAPTER FIVE

The smell of coffee and women's laughter sifted through her sleep with a soft hum. Shayla stretched, extending her arms straight with a shiver and a groan. The heavy arm draped over her side lifted and coasted down her arm.

Her eyes sprung wide and she lurched forward in shock, but John settled her frantic response with another soothing stroke. In a sleep drunken daze, she wiped the drool from the corner of her lips with the palm of her hand.

"Well, good morning." He brushed a strand of hair from her face. "I thought you were going to sleep through the landing."

"Oh, God." His shirt wore a drool mark the size of a half dollar. Shayla turned away from him in humiliation, making another pass at her mouth. "Sorry about your shirt. What happened? Did I fall asleep on you?"

"Don't worry about it. It's my fault anyway. You were sleeping all crooked," — he imitated her discomfort, hanging his head to the side — "so I tried to straighten you out."

A rush of color flooded his cheeks and he looked like a little boy when he grinned. "You snuggled right up next to my chest and we fell asleep that way. I woke up about an hour ago."

Tracy moved through the cabin. She reached into her back pocket, retrieving a picture from her phone. "You were both out cold."

"You didn't put that on Facebook, did you?" Shayla questioned briskly.

"No. We were already warned the whole trip and wedding are top secret."

JC reached her arm through the crack of the seat, showing off her photo of Shayla with her arm sprawled across John's chest. Her face buried against his chest and John was sound asleep with his temple pressed to the top of her head. "This one is so cute! Do you have any idea how hard it is not post these?"

Her lip wrinkled in shock, hit by a wave of embarrassment. Shayla absently rubbed her stiff neck. "Shit."

"What?" He complained teasingly. "You afraid to be seen with me?"

Raking his fingers through his dark mink hair, John arched and stretched like a cat. Straining muscles captured her attention, spreading heat from her cheeks to her toes. Pulling her lower lip into her mouth, she bit down, allowing her gaze to travel from his bulging triceps to strong thighs.

Their gazes met and held.

In order to escape the embarrassment, she stood. "Excuse me."

John twisted, touching his hand to her hip as she scooted by.

The warmth from his handprint on her waist stayed with her all the way to the restroom. Her breathing came hard though a trembling puff of air. She rinsed her mouth and fixed her hair. Catching a whiff of his cologne lingering in the layers of her hair, she closed her eyes and inhaled the yummy scent. "Good lord he's hot."

From out of nowhere, a vision of his pants around his strained thighs while making love to her on the counter popped into her head. Her eyes rolled back as a low ache burned low in her tummy. With every fiber of her being, she wanted to grab him by the wrist and pull him into the stall.

She splashed water on her face and pointed a finger at her longing reflection. "You need to stop."

Putting her hormones in check, she sauntered out to join the others. Each of the Mathews gazed dreamily out their own window as they flew over dozens of small, sun kissed islands. Kneeling on her seat, she gathered with the others in the admiration of the pristine blue waters of the Aegean Sea.

"Have you been to Greece before?" John asked from over her shoulder, nearly resting his chin on her shoulder.

Shayla flinched as the moist heat of his breath set a blazing trail of goose bumps over her entire body. *Mother of pearl what I wouldn't do to feel his gorgeous mouth on my neck.* She managed to shake her head as her words remained strangled in her throat. Inches between their faces, he slowly and tortuously took in every speck of her face as if she were a painting hanging in a gallery. She was worried she might spontaneously combust.

John eased back, buckling his seatbelt, giving her a chance to catch her breath.

Arriving in Greece, Tommy and Tess met them at the airport. Shayla embraced her uncle with open arms, and observed as the Mathews greeted one another with true heartfelt warmth. It was hard not to notice the palpable differences between this family and Mat's. *Huggers.* There was no ceremonial greeting or staunch pretenses, simply adoration.

Tommy's resort-style home perched on a cliff outside the bustling village. The stark white modern home came complete with an amazing view of the Aegean Sea, a pool and enough extra rooms for each of them. Shayla arranged for everyone to stay at an inn after the wedding, but tonight Tommy and Tess insisted everyone stay under one roof, as a *family.* Though she'd always hoped for it, never in a million years did she expect to hear Tommy Clemmins and family in one sentence. This was her uncle's shot at true love and he was going to take it.

It didn't take long to get comfortable. After unpacking, visiting and settling in, Shayla had a minute to think. The azure blue water and afternoon sunshine beckoned from behind the glass wall. She wanted to make the most of the few days on her first trip to Greece. She changed into her bikini, shorts and a sweatshirt, and entered the living room, keys and purse in hand.

"Are you leaving?" Tess asked with a bright inquisitive smile.

Everyone turned, examining her change of clothes.

JC hopped off the sofa first. "Where you going?"

Tracy and John popped their heads up like a prairie gopher popping out of its hole on the Discovery Channel.

Shayla chuckled to herself. She'd hoped for solitude, but judging by the fun-envy growing wider in their eyes, she wouldn't find any isolation right now. "I'm going to the beach. Any takers?"

JC breezed past, hollering from the hallway.

"I'll be ready in five."

"I'm in! And by saying five minutes, she really means ten," Tracy corrected, retreating to her room.

John stood from the sofa, bending to kiss his mother on the cheek. Shayla couldn't help but take in his athletic physique. Her chest tightened as she stared at his firm ass in a pair of jeans that stretched perfectly with each movement of muscle beneath the denim fabric.

She subconsciously stroked her neck as her head cocked slightly for a better view. Lost in her glory daze, John turned and caught her examining his assets. His eyes held a mocking glint as he moseyed straight toward her. Blistering heat layered her cheeks and she dropped her eyes to the floor, letting out a soft nervous giggle.

"I only need two minutes."

The unusually warm weather made for the perfect day for exploring. Tracy and JC talked nonstop on the short drive toward the village. They'd traveled to Greece over the summer and shared everything they loved and learned about the Greek culture, architecture, and mythical history.

Shayla stopped at an overlook where a group of locals gathered at a cliff top.

JC squealed with delight, bolting down the path, not bothering to wait for anyone else. The only words Shayla could make out were Greek gods.

"Greek gods?" Shayla inquired, heading down a narrow path etched along the cliff.

Tracy rolled her eyes. "Our little sister is boy crazy."

"Oh," Shayla managed.

"She doesn't have a lot of boyfriends," Tracy

clarified, sounding as if she didn't want to give the assumption that her sister was easy. "She just—"

"Flirts." John darted an unhappy stare toward JC and a group of four healthy good looking young men.

"I'd say flirting runs in the family." Shayla snickered under her breath. Charm and arrogance ran ramped in her line of work, and John Mathews reeked of it.

"Ha!" Tracy lifted her hand for a high-five. "She's got your number, brother."

He scoffed, throwing his head back with an eye roll. A sexy laugh filled with playful arrogance escaped him. "Not yet she doesn't."

Shayla flushed and for a moment forgot how to breathe. She swallowed. "I don't need to find you a pair of boxing gloves, do I?" she chided.

"Only if you want to take me on."

"I—"

One of the Greek men jumped from the cliff.

"Oh, my God! Did you see that? How far down is that?"

"Twenty-five feet?" John said nonchalantly, obviously surprised at her alarmed reaction.

JC stripped to her bikini before they caught up. Her long caramel hair wisped in the cool breeze as she poised at the brink of the dramatic cliff's edge. Her breathtaking beauty and pleasant, outgoing personality drew people to her like a magnet. The Greek gods strained to keep their eyes from popping out of their heads, unsure of the huge powerful male tagging along behind her.

Relief seemed to wash over the men like the waves below when she introduced John as her brother. In broken English, they gave her instructions on how to time the waves. The boom of energy crashing against the cliff face reverberated up the wall.

"You can't jump off that." Shayla's eyes bulged. "That's way too high, JC."

A dangerous, defiant smile crossed her face. "Ha! Hell yes I'm jumping!"

Groans of complaint came from John and Tracy, each rolling their eyes at Shayla.

"The one thing you don't ever do with JC is use the word can't," Tracy warned, precariously re-treating from the edge.

"That water's got to be fifty-five degrees."

One of the men disagreed, pivoting his hand back and forth. "Sixty-three, maybe sixty-seven de-grees."

Shayla grabbed John by the arm. "You're not seriously going to let her jump, are you?"

John approached to the rim of the black jag-ged rock, peering over to assess the level of danger.

JC stood beside him, waiting for his response.

He shrugged, giving JC all the encourage-ment she needed.

She threw her hands in the air. "Woo-hoo! I'm going."

The young men, more interested in JC's strik-ing beauty and string bikini than the two story drop, gathered at her side. Excitement filled her smile as she plotted her jump, oblivious to the effect she had on them. Timing the waves perfectly, she jumped, screaming the whole way down until she hit the cold water.

Another man joined in the craziness. He backed up fifteen feet, running down the path and hurling himself over the ledge.

"You coming?" John taunted, tugging his

shirt over his head and handing it to Tracy.

Momentarily speechless, Shayla let her gaze linger over his perfectly defined pecs. "Me? I'm not jumping off that. I'm afraid of heights!"

"What?" John scoffed in surprise, resting his hands on his hips. "That's not what Tom said. He told us you jumped out of an airplane for your twenty-first birthday."

She grimaced at the memory.

"He talked about you a lot over Thanksgiving." Tracy nodded. "That's why we've been looking forward to meeting you."

Preconceived guilt pinged through her. Shayla had been dreading meeting Tess's kids because of the way they'd harshly judged her uncle. She realized her opinion of them was made in the same haste judgment. "I suppose he forgot to mention the fact he dangled a pretty big carrot in front of me. He sent me to a personal awareness retreat, and if I graduated," —she curled her fingers into quotes— "he'd buy me a new car."

Their eyes widened in surprise.

"He didn't force me," she clarified. "He would've got me the car regardless. I felt so damn empowered by the end of the week, I had a *Wonder Woman* moment and jumped."

"Well, this is nothing compared to jumping from an airplane a mile high in the sky." John's fingers hooked in the band of his trunks, dipping them lower around his lean waist.

"I...I don't think you should go." As Shayla's eyes followed the descent of John's drawstring, a riff of personal awareness zinged through her. Trepidation mixed with yearning. Her tongue seemed to be tied in the knot of his trunks. She backed away, shaking her head. "I can't, it's way too high."

"Come on, you big chicken!" JC beckoned from the chilly blue water. The gurgle of sea swells crashing against the jagged rocks below mixed with echoes of JC's shrieks of joy.

"Are you jumping too?" Shayla asked Tracy.

"No way. Those two are the adrenaline junkies," Tracy validated. She held her arm out offering to hold Shayla's belongings. "They take after our dad and I'm more like my mom. I'll meet you on the beach."

Anxiety pumped through her veins and she paced like a caged lion. *Making the most of every opportunity means stepping out of your comfort zone*, she repeated silently.

"Do you really think I would let my sister jump if there was any chance of getting hurt?" John held out his hand. "I'll take care of you," he offered in a throaty voice sounding more like a heated promise than fact.

Cocky! Before she had time to give it another thought she kicked off her shoes, shimmied out of her shorts and grabbed her sweatshirt by the hem, pulling it over her head and giving it to Tracy. *You can do this!*

Anxiety kicked in and Shayla's chest heaved laboriously. Holding her hands in front of her tummy, she squeezed one hand then the other, balling them into tight fists.

"Great bikini." John took two steps toward her. His center finger grazed along the thin brown strap of her swimsuit, lazily exploring her collarbone.

The rough texture of his skin made her shiver. She found herself listing forward, close enough to smell the sweet scent of his minty breath. Alarmed by her own reaction to his touch, Shayla blinked repeatedly, staring upward into his gaze.

"You look beautiful." An impish grin twitched at the corner of his mouth. "Your freckles really stand out in the sunshine."

The amused gleam in his eye astounded her, spreading heat all the way to her toes. Self-consciously, she touched the faint freckles dusting her cheeks and nose.

His smile turned full.

"You really expect that to work?"

"God, I hope so," John teased, gathering her hands in his. "Flattery is supposed to go a long way. It should work for a twenty-foot jump."

"Hey!" JC's lively voice echoed up the face of the rock. "Are you guys gonna make out or jump?"

"That would be your call." His eyes blazed both in invitation and challenge. "Wonder Woman."

The breeze shifted, filling her nostrils with the scent of his sweet breath. Tunnel vision set in, but she wasn't slipping into a fading black hole. Shayla's vision fell into the depths of his and held. Her lip caught between her teeth.

The tip of his finger turned circles on the band of her ring, blanching his humor. "I'll count to three."

Shayla shut her eyes tight, drawing in a deep breath of determination. *Be brave.* She clutched John's hand. She opened her eyes and nodded. As they approached the edge, he released her hand and she hissed in a frightened breath.

"It's okay." He wiped the sweat from her hand on his shorts, only to tighten his grip around her fingers. "One, two, three."

They jumped from the edge.

Screams of exhilaration rang in her ears, sounding nothing like her own voice. Their hands parted before they hit the water. Plunging into the blue, she felt the bite of cold water rush over her flesh. Her descent slowed upon impact as adrenaline surged through her, stealing her breath. Shayla swam to the surface.

They emerged from the cold water with shrieks of ecstasy.

"Nice job!" He beamed with approval, giving her a high-five.

His praise made her bubbly inside. "That was awesome! What a rush!"

Tracy waited for them as they trudged onto the beach, and JC headed up the trail ready for round two. Shayla jumped twice, but John and JC jumped four times before the sun lowered over the horizon.

JC's new friends offered to share their towels, water, snacks and, in a show of male bravado, jokingly argued over who got to ask her to dinner. Wearing the face of a dejected puppy, she begrudgingly declined their invitation. Her spirits seemed to lift as she plodded through the sand following the tall dreamy one of the bunch toward his car. She held up a finger, signaling her siblings she'd be right back.

"Is she giving him her number?" Shayla asked Tracy.

Tracy nodded, divulging the information quietly so John couldn't hear. "JC still talks to three boys in Italy she met over the summer. She's already planning our trip back. I had to bribe her with coffee every day for a month to get her to go to Europe with me. Now, she wants to stay longer and take part in the travel arrangements."

John stood at the water's edge, his feet buried

in the black sand while talking to two of the other jumpers. There were enough hard bodies and sex appeal between the three men to make any woman within eyesight stop and ogle, but Shayla couldn't take her eyes off John. It wasn't only his striking looks capturing her attention; his confidence and genuine ease of his smile filled her with warmth.

Hiding behind her sunglasses, she stared on as he shook the water from his hair and ran his fingers through the short thick strands of silk. Each well-defined muscle took its turn center stage. Shayla crossed one leg over the other, hoping to ease the jolts of thunder striking her inner thighs. Chill bumps rose high on his skin, constricting his dark nipples when the breeze hit his wet body. Her breath fractured when he shifted slightly and exposed a full frontal of his wet trucks clinging to his body.

"Can't say I blame my little sister. There is something special about European men," Tracy interjected, enjoying the beachside view.

JC jogged back with a smile plastered to her face. "He's HOT!" she boasted, flapping a piece of paper with his number written on it. She leaned in closer to Shayla, peering toward the men standing along the border of the incoming surf. "Which one do you think is cute?"

Shayla's mouth opened and closed. The scorch of embarrassment climbed up her neck. *Shit!* Her hungry gaze and smirk fell to the sand. Both girls snickered and shook their heads as if they'd seen it a million times. Shayla had no doubt the Mathews house was the high school spot for sleepovers. The entire family hit the gene pool jackpot.

They spent the late afternoon meandering down cobbled streets of the quaint village. The close connection between John and his sisters was unlike anything Shayla had ever encountered between siblings. They genuinely enjoyed each other and their humorous camaraderie kept her laughing.

Their father died of a heart attack a year before their mother met Tommy, and John filled every inch of the head of household position. As they perused the streets, men who took notice of his sisters or Shayla were tolerated, but John's mere presence kept any strangers at bay. There wasn't one catcall or indecent gesture, not even so much as an unwanted prolonged stare. He didn't act like a bulldog bodyguard, but his rugged exterior carried a presence of sureness and conviction, strong enough to dominate any male. His sisters seemed used to his powerful persona, but it sparked a new sense of safety for Shayla.

John led them through the streets with ease, constantly placing his hand on the small of her back. He did this to his sisters as well, but as the afternoon wore on, his hand lingered longer and longer on Shayla's back. She found herself comforted by his touch, almost leaning into him when they spoke. The rough calluses on his palms snagged at the material of her shirt. Shayla reached for his hand, rubbing her thumb over the scratchy surface of his palm. "Tommy mentioned you were in construction. What do you do?"

"I'm part owner in my dad's construction company." He remained still, allowing her to hold his hand. The crescents of his lashes shadowed his cheeks. "These are from mountain biking."

Her thumbs continued to turn circles over the coarse skin. The setting sun deepened the fresh bronze coloring on his face, accentuating the vibrant green of his eyes. She found herself mesmerized by the color and texture of the skin on his neck. "You took over the company after your father died?"

"Yes, but it wasn't quite that simple. I've worked for my dad as far back as I can remember." He smiled with a sense of pride. "I had to earn my spot at the top. The other partners bought my mom out after he died, and I worked hard to prove myself. They made me a partner three months ago."

"Congratulations." She raised her brows and smiled sweetly. "I'm sure your dad would be proud of you."

Tracy clasped her bother by the shoulder. "Yes, Dad would be very proud."

Tracy was the quietest of the three. She helped Shayla pick out the perfect wedding gift for Tom and Tess, while JC picked out all the hot-blooded Greeks in the near vicinity.

Tommy and Tess met them for dinner at a café along the water's edge. The owner greeted her uncle and his family with gracious, warm smiles, swiftly ushering them to a private table along the terrace. The stark white stucco ignited with colors of cobalt blue and magenta pink mixed with a splash of sunny yellow. A plush throw draped over each chair and gas heaters warmed the chill of the evening air.

Greece reeked of love and desire, and the seduction of the atmosphere was arresting. Even the local dishes on the menu were crammed with adjectives like lust, kisses, breasts, smoldering and volcanic. Sitting across the table from John, Shayla threatened to erupt with fiery passion at any unsuspecting moment as conversation carried on around her. Each time he smiled through dinner, her spirits soared with shameless delight.

Lights from catamarans and luxury yachts dotted the serene setting as the darkness overtook the sinking sun. Shayla closed her eyes, her head slant to the side, listening to the echoes of music and voices carrying over the cool moist evening air. She pulled in a deep breath of salty air. Every inch of her mind melted into the moment as it absorbed all that Greece had to offer.

John rested his hand on her forearm. "Are you going to fall asleep again?"

Her eyes remained shut, and she basked in the bliss of his hand sparking energy in her skin. "No. I'm not tired at all. I'm just so relaxed."

Searching her memory, she wondered if she'd ever felt this content. She opened her eyes, peering out at the horizonless expanse of water. "I don't remember the last time I felt this calm."

"Me either." Their gazes briefly fixed on each other. John's hand drifted down her arm, jiggling her finger that adorned a diamond accessory before releasing her hand.

"I suggest you enjoy it while you can, Shay."

She startled at the sound of her uncle's voice.

"You'll be busy when you get home."

Sheer insanity. Placing her hands in her lap, Shayla grimaced at his firm warning of the hell coming over the next few months. The paparazzi would call an all out war on Tommy and Tess's wedding. The Wild West antics would be frightening and precarious. On top of that, Mat would be waiting for her and an answer.

Leaving the café, they strolled along the dimly lit cobbled streets. White buildings gave stark contrast to the volcanic cliffside. November brought the off-season, giving her uncle the ability to roam the streets freely without too much of a hassle. This would never happen state side and Shayla enjoyed being in public without fans or press breathing down their neck.

Most of the merchants closed up shop early, leaving only a few shops and a coffee shop to peruse. Shayla veered off alone, finding her way to the end of a narrow corridor. Small balconies hovered above tables set for two. Potted plants and menus written in chalk showing off the day's fresh catch and specials lined the sidewalks.

Reaching the end of the passage, she leaned against the lava rock wall, gazing out at the moonbeam igniting the entire cove with its attendance. Caught in a trance, Shayla's heart measured in painful beats. Mat represented everything she dreamed of as a little girl, but her list of requirements for prince charming had changed over the last few months. Even though Mat had all of the qualities to make a good man, that didn't make him the right man.

Tears pooled in her eyes. She buried her face in the palm of her hands, blotting the corner of her damp eyes. With each minute that ticked by, her reflection of their relationship became clearer. Dread of the next few weeks quickly crawled into her mind, wiping out the serene view in front of her.

Quiet footsteps resonated through the corridor from behind. There was no need to turn, she knew it'd be John.

"Wow," he whispered.

Resting his forearms on the black pumice stone, he stared in awe. Intense energy passed between them. His gaze turned to her ring, yet he remained wordless.

The tiniest pebble of a stone adorning her finger suddenly became as big as moon hovering above the caldron in the distance.

She felt the need to explain, but the details caught in her throat, leaving her unable to speak. She cleared her throat and turned to him. "I…I never thought I'd find this place so magical. You know what I mean? You see pictures, but they don't do it justice."

"The view is…mysterious." His keen stare bore into the depths of her soul. "Breathtaking."

A sexy smile threatened to expose itself at the corner of his mouth until her tongue slipped across her bottom lip, nervously tugging it between her teeth. His breath caught and his stare turned hungry. "Why, umm, has it taken you so long to visit Greece?" he stammered, breaking the hum of sensual energy between them.

"I've always wanted to travel here. I just never made the time. Tommy's only had this place a few years." She didn't want to admit or explain that Mat wouldn't come with her. He was afraid he'd be bored.

"How long have you worked for Tom?"

"I started working for him right out of high school, part-time until I finished college."

"Did you grow up in California?" he asked, his tone permeated with intrigue as if it would be the first of dozens of questions he needed to ask.

"No, I grew up in Kentucky." She smiled, but a bit of sadness forged its way into her voice. "Tommy took me in when I showed up on his doorstep."

"You just showed up?" John's eyes flickered warily. "His brother is your father, right?"

A chill skittered up her spine from the tenderness in his tone, tugging at her insides. She never spoke of her father. Emotions she put to rest years ago flooded over her unexpectedly. She sniffed back the burning sting pricking her nose, threatening to turn to tears. Shayla bowed her head with a slight nod. "My father isn't anything like Tommy. The two of them haven't gotten along in years. He's not a nice man."

She sensed concern rising in his silence.

"Define not nice." The uneasiness collecting in the vibrations of his voice closed like a fist around her heart, pulling her to him.

"He's an alcoholic," she admitted, raising her gaze to meet his. She couldn't explain the comfort and security she felt merely standing next to him. There was just something about John that made her trust him. She continued without a second thought. "And abusive."

His face stiffened. A sea of anger brewed in his eyes. They held a thousand questions in just one look. "Was he abusive to you?"

"My mother took the brunt of it." Shayla found herself unable to stop the train wreck of a story spilling from her lips. "I guess I've never really forgiven her for staying with him. Or for not sticking up for me."

"Parents are supposed to protect their children." The muscles in his neck tensed. A murderous grumble resonated deep in his chest, rising above the crashing surf in the dark distance. "Your family should be the people you can trust the most. Not the ones who give you nightmares."

John protected his family. He defended his mother against one of the most famous men in the world without giving her uncle's notoriety a second thought.

"Not everyone is as protective as you." She managed a smile while brushing the dampness from her face.

"Your uncle is. He talks about you like you're his own daughter." A curious frown puckered between his brows. "Did you run away?"

Shayla shook her head. "When I was sixteen, Tommy came back to Kentucky for my grandma's funeral. We talked a lot and I confided in him. I remember thinking, how can he be so nice and my father be so awful? He told me if I ever needed *anything* I could come to him. I don't know what went down between them the day of my grandma's funeral. Tommy would never say, but I suspect he threatened my father." She added quietly, "I think it almost killed him to leave me there."

Hostility hung on him, as he tenderly brushed the slick of wetness from her jaw with the back of his finger. "What happened?"

"After I graduated, things had gotten really bad one night. He started drinking early in the morning, and by late afternoon, the screaming and yelling had hit full tilt. I locked myself in my room when he started waving a gun around." Her mind sifted through the ugly memory. "I could hear him beating up my mom, and before I realized what I was doing, I cracked him over the head with a frying pan."

"You hit him with a frying pan?" he asked with wide eyes.

"It kind of plays through my memory like a cartoon." She cringed, turning her finger in a circle near her temple. "I shoved all I could fit into a backpack, taped a goodbye note to his bottle of vodka, and stepped right over the top of him as I was leaving. I would have asked my mother to come with me, but I knew she would never leave him."

"You walked out the door and never went back?"

"It wouldn't surprise me if Tommy has been paying my father off to stay away from me. I'm thankful if he does." Shayla released a shaky sigh of relief. She'd never confided in Mat this way. She found it too shameful to share her story with him, and he never bothered to dig deeper into her life. She almost got the feeling Mat knew exactly how she had been raised, but never wanted to pry or expose the sad truth of it. Or maybe he knew it would hurt his mother's campaign.

"That takes a lot of courage." John stared at her with a prideful glow.

A rewarding smile replaced her tears. "I caught a train and showed up at the gate outside my uncle's house, but he wasn't home. I waited for hours in the pouring rain. I was soaked to the bone and freezing cold. I finally decided to climb the gate." She spread her arms high and wide. "Have you seen his place in Malibu? It's like Fort Knox."

His mood lightened when she smiled. John shook his head, enthralled in her story. "No, not yet. What happened? Did security show up? Throw you jail?"

"Worse! I was half way over the wall and the old lady next door pointed a shotgun at my butt!"

They both laughed. Her stiff shoulders loosened as she calmed down.

He cocked his pretend shotgun, taking aim at her ass. "Nice neighbor."

"Oh, my God, wait till you see her! She's about five feet tall with white hair pulled back in a bun and ornery as the day is long."

"Note to self: never jump Tom's wall." John pointed his finger, mocking her accent. "I think I just heard a bit of Kentucky in there somewhere."

"There you two are!" JC waved frantically from half way down the corridor. "Come on, it's time to go! The Jacuzzi is calling!"

John waved from the shadows. "We're coming!" Glancing down at Shayla with a hopeful grin, he asked, "Jacuzzi?"

"I'm in." They passed by the tables and she stopped, giving the seam of his shirt a quick yank. "Thanks for listening. I never talk about my father. Most people don't know anything about my past."

"Oh, we're just getting started." Sexual tension streamed along in a constant undercurrent.

Perspiration gathered at her nape as her gaze locked on the pulse throbbing at the base of his neck, slamming her with a brand of desire she'd never encountered. "We are?"

"Oh yeah. I want to hear the end of the story. Obviously your ass is still fully intact." He leaned back taking in the view of her derriere. "I want to hear more about the gun-toting granny who lives next door."

"Okay." Shayla didn't understand why this man put such a spell on her, but she was certain she'd tell him anything.

CHAPTER SIX

"The thermometer reads one hundred and two degrees," Tracy affirmed as Shayla poked her toe into the hot water.

Shayla sighed, easing the rest of her body into the rolling bubbles. "This feels incredible."

"It's heavenly." Tracy's head tilted back over the edge of the Jacuzzi. "Do you think Tom would let us stay here for vacation?"

"I'm sure he would."

She opened one eye. "As long as you don't bring friends over. Tommy's very protective of his privacy. We'll have to go over a few things, a lot of things, before you get back home. We should all enjoy the moment, because it's gonna be insane when this hits the media."

Tracy sat tall, concern etched across her face. "How insane?"

"Envision a pack of wolves hunting a very cleaver rabbit." She warned. "Full on crazy!"

"I'm up for crazy!" JC interjected, sashaying toward the Jacuzzi with a bottle of wine and four clear plastic cups.

"Does Mom know you're drinking wine?" Tracy's question rang with authority.

"I'm of age in Europe," JC snickered. She passed a glass of wine to each of them, descending into the steam next to her sister. "Besides, Mom and Tom already went to bed."

Shayla scooted lower in her seat, allowing the jets to work magic on her sore neck.

"So!" JC wiggled her brows, lifting her cup to cheers them. "How crazy is crazy? Are they going to be on the cover of every magazine? Entertainment TV? Our local news?"

"Yes." The pounding jet hit a tight muscle, causing Shayla to wince. "Not to mention complaints made by the millions of women who will be crying into their morning cup of coffee."

Tracy's expression bounced between uneasy worry and sheer panic.

"It's okay, the other millions will be saying, *Finally! It's about time!*"

JC giggled dismissively.

"Life will be completely different from now on, absolutely wonderful in some ways and a complete pain in the ass in others. The paparazzi are like predators. It's easy to get caught up in the bright shiny lights and friendly faces, but make no mistake"—Shayla looked her in the eye, needing her to understand the gravity of the situation—"these people are not nice. Every single eye roll and swear word is bound to get caught on tape and God forbid you give the finger to the paparazzi."

"I don't know if my mom is ready for this." Concern deepened in Tracy's blue eyes.

"I'm not trying to scare you. Tommy will keep her safe," Shayla assured. "I just want you to understand the magnitude of the situation. He has a lot of pull and everyone owes him favors, including the paparazzi. I'm sure he'll call in every one of them owed to him. Plus he has bodyguards most of the time."

Both the girls' eyes widened.

"*We* might need a bodyguard?" Tracy's finger wafted between her and her sister.

"You won't even know they are there. He wants to keep this as painless as possible, but safety will be his number one concern. In this business you have to take what's thrown at you, deal with it as it comes and keep your wits about you."

Tracy clutched to her cup. "What the hell does that mean?"

"That means we won't know the extent of the storm until we're in the middle of the hurricane." Shayla crossed her arms over her chest, allowing the pulsing hot water to beat against the knot hidden behind her blade. "You didn't like my uncle dating your mom at first. Why?"

Stunned by Shayla's candor, the girls faced one another.

JC shrugged, pointing at her sister. "Hey, I had no problem with him. Tracy and John are the ones who didn't like him."

"Are you talking about me?" John's rich voice sent jitters down her back. His rugged frame silhouetted by the moon hanging in the dark sky, he poured a glass of wine for himself offering to top off the girls.

"Yeah." Without hesitation, JC chimed in, "Explain why didn't you like Tom when you first met him?"

His face sobered in the shadows, tilting his head from side to side. John stepped into the Jacuzzi slowly sinking down beside Shayla, one row of rippled muscle at a time. "Let's just say his reputation precedes him."

"Your perception of Tommy came from the media. Most of what you read isn't true or is at least highly embellished," Shayla clarified. "The paparazzi are toxic and they're not concerned about how much truth there is to a story, as long as it sells. Unfortunately, you're not going to like everything you read or hear, but you have to learn to ignore it instead of reacting to the lies."

She heeded the direct warning to John and JC.

John and Tracy glanced at each other, worry gathering on their faces.

"He wants to keep everything wrapped up in a perfect package with nice tight bow, but in reality, their wedding will be one of the biggest stories of the year. But…he is very good at damage control. Genius by Hollywood's standards. "

A weighted hush fell over them, soaking in the life change they hadn't fully considered.

"Wow." Even JC seemed robbed of words…for a minute. "Speaking of weddings, why do you wear an engagement ring on the wrong hand?"

"JC," Tracy snapped, nipping a warning to her little sister.

"What?" JC shrugged innocently. "Oh, come on. We're gonna be family tomorrow. It's not like I'm the only one that's curious." She teased sarcastically. "Inquiring minds want to know."

John lifted her hand to inspect the rock on her finger.

Shayla's stare targeted John.

"Hey, don't pin this on me." John lifted one shoulder with a nod of admittance. "I am curious though."

His reaction captured his sisters' attention. JC

shot Tracy an *I told you so* nod.

A powerful rush of emotions made her throat ache with discomfiture. She stumbled through her explanation. "I'm not engaged. He…Mat proposed over Thanksgiving."

John remained quiet and relinquished her hand into the effervescent bubbles.

Shayla got the distinct feeling he was patiently waiting, waiting for JC to fill in the gaps.

Right on queue JC snickered, "And? Why the ring if you're not engaged?"

"I didn't have an answer."

"So, you're wearing the ring on the right hand while you consider the proposal?" Her forwardness bordered on brash, yet she spun it with a sincere innocence.

Shayla's stomach twisted from the tension gathering between her and John. He'd been eyeing her ring from the moment they met. She could tell he wanted to ask about it back at the wall, and oddly enough, she had the unfaltering urge to explain, but was interrupted by his sister. "Basically."

"How long have you been dating?"

"Almost two years."

"Two years?" JC slapped the water and jumped to her feet in the center of the Jacuzzi, throwing her hands to the heavens. "This is why I only date."

Shayla startled at her exuberance.

"Boyfriends are too hard to get rid of and the business of breaking up is awful. Having a boyfriend is like having an uncommitted commitment."

"Here we go, another round of JC's dating philosophy." John drowned his mockery in his glass of wine.

"Come again? What do you mean?" Shayla hung on JC's every word, her spry youthful spirit filled with ripened wisdom.

"If you're committed to a boyfriend then you're not dating, right?"

"Right," Shayla agreed.

"If you've been dating for over a year and you're still not sure if he's the one, then you, chica, are burning daylight!"

"It's really not that simple."

John added, "Yeah, lil sister, it's not that easy when politics are involved."

Even though his tone was pleasant, the words sliced through the water, jabbing at Shayla's heart. He stared straight at her, watching carefully to see if his words stung.

They did.

JC continued. "Actually, it is that simple. Boyfriends who aren't right for you are like having a huge piece of luggage strapped to your back. Life is too damn short. Cut the relationship ripcord and date."

"Don't listen to her." Tracy shot her sister a warning. "She's anti-marriage."

"I am not anti-marriage. I simply think dating makes more sense. Breaking up is exhausting and sucks the life out of you. Typically it's the same routine. You try to break up, he convinces you to give it another shot. You're simply prolonging the inevitable."

Stunned by her absoluteness, Shayla blinked. The reality of her statement seeped into her pores with the steam floating at the surface. She glanced at Tracy for input.

Tracy interjected, "I think people come into

our lives for a reason, a season or a lifetime. Maybe he's more of a reason than a lifetime, you know, but it's possible you're supposed to grow from the relationship. But JC's right about the ripcord, life is too short."

"If you're not sold on him yet, how much longer are you willing to wait? Time is rushing by! Mr. Right could be next to you at any given moment."

Shayla's gaze drifted to the man at her right. Their eyes met with such force, it licked through her body like a hot flame.

"How come he's not here for the wedding?"

Her prolonged silence filled the cool evening air with curiosity. "I didn't tell him. Mat thinks I'm working."

JC's brow raised to a point. Her mouth opened, forming a big O fish mouth. "You can't trust him enough to bring him to the wedding?"

Tracy shot a soft elbow to her sister's ribs, giving her a quick shake of the head.

JC twisted her finger in a locking motion in front of her lips. "Chicka-lock. I won't say another word."

Colored with shame, Shayla felt even more foolish watching a light of understanding flash across John's eyes as blatant as the moon's shimmering stripe etching across the surface of the sea. "I couldn't risk telling anyone about the wedding. It's not like he would tell anyone on purpose, but if he accidentally let it slip out—"

"You don't need to explain," John said.

The conversation swirled on around her as Shayla sank deeper in her thoughts. She couldn't ignore the choice she needed to make when she returned to California. Her answer to Mat leaned further and further to denial, yet she wasn't certain. She was certain, however, of the sensual awareness she felt for the man sitting beside her. The tenderness in his voice and smile made her dizzy. Shayla wanted to know everything about him, and Lord knows she wanted to reach out and touch every inch of him. Guilt mixed with longing. Her heart thrashed wildly inside her chest the closer she crept to John.

By the time the girls said goodnight and retreated inside, she and John sat so close their thighs brushed. The sensual scent of him drifted across the water and ignited her senses. Her body ached painfully, the desire building like a storm, nearly unbearable.

Neither spoke, seeming unsure of what to say. The sultry air eddied around them like dense fog.

"Don't let my little sister's dating philosophy or twenty questions upset you." He splashed his face with hot water and scrubbed his fingers through his dark hair. Irritability cloaked him like the sudsy bubbles. "I'm sure you have your reasons for waiting."

"How did you—"

"I asked Tom."

"Oh." She nodded. The fact he inquired about her sent a rush of delight through her. "JC's right, you know. She just has the courage to say it like it is."

He lifted a dark brow, looking amused and encouraged. "Believe me, it's a blessing and a curse."

"I just expected it to be so different," she confided, unable to stop the words from spilling out of her mouth. It was dangerous to be so close to him, to open up and share her feelings about Mat and his proposal. She felt safe with John. She could tell him anything, and he wouldn't judge her. "I thought if a person had the right qualities and a kind character, everything would fall into place."

He pumped his fist, squirting water into the air, ciphering her words. "I guess I believe more in Fate than a check list. My parents always taught us that everything in life happens for a reason."

Sorrow lingered speaking of his parents. "One of my father's favorite quotes was *Life isn't measured by the number of breaths we take, but by the moments that take our breath away.* He just refused to waste a day."

"Destiny." She nodded absently, closing her eyes and sinking lower onto the jet.

John reached around her shoulder, pulling her through the water so the back of her thighs rested against his knees. She stiffened in surprise, attempting to plant her feet on the bottom of the Jacuzzi, but buoyancy made her float onto the edge of his lap. His strong fingers manipulated the sore muscles on her neck and shoulder.

"John, you don't have to…" Shayla could barely speak, attempting to decline the back rub. Within seconds she melted into his touch. "Oh."

"Shhh. You'll like it," he assured, both hands working jointly up the blades of her back, applying pressure in slow wide circles. "I understand Tracy's theory that people come into our lives for a reason, a season or lifetime."

"You mean to teach us something?" Arousal coiled around her as his hands moved in strong gliding strokes, searching out the sore muscles. Time slowed and her breathing came in deep long breaths.

The smell of his wet hair clung to her senses. She could taste the scent of him.

"Yes. Then there's those friends you get together with a few times a year, but it feels like you saw them yesterday."

"What about lifetimers?" she questioned in a hush. His rough-worked hands coasted downward to the middle of her back, slowly and effortlessly exploring one side then the other with strong rotations.

"Well, I guess those people would be the ones you love enough to endure a lifetime."

The quiet night sky fell over them. The intimate act of his hands on her flesh brought clarity to her surroundings. The chilled air felt crisp on her damp face and her chest burned with building sentiment. Calluses on the pads of his hand added to his masculinity, and the involuntary tightening of muscles deep in her center threatened to erupt at any moment.

John swept her sodden hair over one shoulder, the texture of his fingers making her tremble. "Feel good, Shay?"

His breath tickled her ear.

She trembled with acute awareness. Shayla knew exactly how his lips would feel on her neck. The heat, the tenderness, the urgency. "Yes," she whimpered softly, dropping her chin to her chest, giving him full access to her nape.

His hands dipped to the silk skin at her waist.

John adjusted her bottom further back onto the middle of his thighs. Her legs dangled freely in the water. As he gripped her hips for steadiness, a vision flashed through her of what it would be like to make love to him. Shayla could feel the ghost of his hands exploring her body, bringing her to life, the rise and fall of his hips, and his mouth exploring her skin.

Reveling in the power of his thighs beneath her, she mindlessly squirmed backward. Her breathing came in shallow pants. She wanted to feel him, needed to know if he desired her.

John remained fixed, purposely not allowing to her to ease onto his lap.

His right hand drifted down her arm, exposing her hand and ring from the water. He brushed a few loose wet ribbons of her hair from her neck, grazing his lips over her shoulder. "So technically, where does that leave you, Shay? Right now?"

She molded her back to his rigid chest. The pounding of his heart sent a zing of excitement through her, an overwhelming feeling of connection and intimacy for a man she barely knew.

"Technically, we're on a break." Her tongue felt heavy and dry. "I told him I would have an answer when I get home."

After a long pause, he lifted her from his lap and turned her to face him. "And do you have an answer yet?"

The cool night air drew steam from her hot skin. She couldn't find the strength to reply. Fine hairs on her arm stood up as his dark eyes bore into hers with hope. Her nose wrinkled as she tried to hold back the tears. Her chest felt heavy with regret and she didn't realize she was crying. "I'm sorry."

The lines near his eyes crinkled in discouragement. "Well, what are you crying for, Shay?"

He pulled her between his thighs and wrapped his arms around her, stroking her wet hair.

She sniffed, shaking her head once.

"It's a simple yes or no answer that only alters the entire rest of your life." He tried to make her smile, but his was voice laced with pity and frustration.

She draped her arms around his neck, laying her cheek on his shoulder. "I don't know why I'm crying. I never cry."

"I don't smell like an onion, do I?"

"What? No." Shayla pulled away, getting a peek at his smiling face. "I want to tell you my answer is no, but I'm not totally certain. I need to give him my answer before I can..." Her gaze caught on his mouth. "Before I could..."

He hauled her close, their faces a mere inches apart. His playful grin broadened. "So you do like me."

She put on her best poker face for a whole three seconds before looking skyward with a huge grin. "You're okay."

John released her and jolted out of his seat. "Do you think you can fly to California, give him your answer, and be back before the wedding tomorrow?"

Stepping out of the Jacuzzi, he grabbed a fluffy white towel and wrapped it around his waist, holding another one open to swathe around her wet body.

Shayla appreciated his effort to keep the atmosphere humorous. "I think it might take longer than that."

"I could go with you." He grabbed another towel and scrubbed it through her hair as if they'd know each other for years. "The flight back would be…very turbulent."

His low voice reverberated through her like a sweet caress.

Shayla stared at his dense collarbone heaving with each breath. Her gaze wondered up the textured skin of his throat, heat spreading everywhere when their eyes met and held. She swallowed hard.

"I suppose a text denial would be out of the question?" he joked, but seriousness dripped to his humor.

Overwhelmed with a multitude of emotions, she began to say something, but the words wouldn't come. "I—that wouldn't be—I "

He took careful measures, inspecting her reaction. "It's okay. I understand."

"I don't know how you could understand when even I don't understand." Her words trailed off into the darkness.

Making their way inside, temptation to try to explain her feelings lurked at each passing doorway. They remained subdued until reaching her bedroom door. She trembled all over. In an act of comfort, John eased her into his arms.

Shayla went limp. Standing right outside her bedroom in the arms of a man she desperately wanted to get to know put her in a very dangerous position.

He gently swayed back and forth, his embrace warm and loving.

The desire to respond to his affection was unbearable, her heart working in fast frantic beats. *God, he smells good.* Unable to resist, she relaxed into him further, resting her cheek on the hard planes of his chest.

"Do you think we can go on a date when we get back?" John asked in a whisper. His mouth brushed over her damp hair. "If you're not engaged, that is?"

Her thoughts shattered into a million possibilities and she nodded hotly. "Yes—"

He lowered his mouth inches from hers. The earthy oak bouquet of the wine still lingered on his breath.

"My reputable morals have reached their max capacity, so unless you want me to turn on a hot shower, take you to bed, and tuck you in, you should go now. I don't think I can take much more before I kiss you."

"Okay," Shayla mumbled incoherently, turning blindly toward the door and opening it.

He patted her on the bottom. "Good night, Shay."

"Night," she managed to utter before he closed the door.

Slumping against the door and placing her ear to the wood, she listened to his footsteps fade down the hallway. She remained that way for minutes, half-hoping he'd return. The warm imprint of his arms wrapped securely around her filled her heart with need and contentment. Ambling toward the shower, she noticed her phone lying on the bedside table remained dark. *No blinking green light.* She didn't bother checking. Mat hadn't called.

Dragging herself into the shower, she allowed the cascade of scalding water to wash over her. Shayla couldn't disregard the reality and overwhelming happiness of being encompassed in the arms of a man she barely knew. He emanated a feeling of joy that was foreign to her.

Shayla gazed aimlessly into the mirror, running the hair dryer over her wet mane, dwelling on letting John walk away. She felt like she was spinning out of control, yet she'd never possessed such a grasp on her awareness of a man.

She stared down at the engagement ring adorning her right ring finger. Emotions of deep regret and keen desire and horrible guilt churned through her thoughts.

Shayla needed more than a list of comfortable qualities. She needed unspoken feelings of security and passion. Shayla slipped the ring from her finger and tucked it out of sight in her jewelry box.

Mentally exhausted, she rubbed lotion over her skin before slipping into her white cotton camisole and lace panties. Pulling back the layers of comfy blankets on her bed, she noticed a shadow from beneath her bedroom door out of the corner of her eye. A nervous shiver skittered down her back. *John.*

CHAPTER SEVEN

A fever of hot molten lava raced across her skin, instantly turning her hands damp. Shayla nervously waved her wet hands in the air, watching the shadow pace outside her door in the lit hallway. Flutters danced through her tummy. She tiptoed to the door and silently rested her hand on the handle.

The pacing came to a halt.

A smile curled on the corner of her mouth. John could see her shadow beneath to door as well. With only a solid piece of wood between them, her composure fractured, sending tingling sensations to the tender area between her thighs.

Her heartbeat drummed so erratically in her ears she could barely hear the soft tapping on the door. Shayla eased the door open a few inches, trying to conceal her smile. "Hey," she said softly. "What's up?"

John lifted a brow, amused by the double meaning of her words. His arm flexed a little, pushing the door open a bit further, stretching the thin t-shirt snug over the hard lines of his torso. His gaze wandered keenly from her toes to her face with utter slowness, settling on her eyes. He squinted ambiguously. "I want to ask you something."

Engrossed in the fresh scent of his skin and damp hair at his nape, she gripped the handle for support. "Okay," she panted breathlessly.

John stepped across the threshold, clasping her hands in his. "Stay with me?"

Her thoughts scattered and she dropped her gaze to the floor.

He waited until Shayla could bring herself to look at him. "Don't act like you don't feel the connection between us."

"I do, but—"

"Come with me." John took a step back, gently tugging on her hands, beckoning her toward the hallway.

In a daze, she took a quick scan of her cami and panties barely covering her backside. Shayla reached for a white silk cover-up hanging on the back of the door.

John snatched the robe from her hands and tossed it onto her bed, shaking his head. "Please don't put that on. You look absolutely breathtaking."

His compliment made her heart swoon. She poked her head into the hall. "But—"

He pulled her into his arms and Shayla squealed in surprise at his powerful embrace. The rough texture of one of his palms traveling down the small of her back and cupping her exposed cheek made her gasp. His smile widened into a slow burn of desire, igniting a fire in her belly. Every fine hair on her body stood at attention.

She swallowed hard. "I can't make any promises."

Taking her hand, John led her down the hall to his room.

Standing at his door, John caressed her arms, pausing before turning the handle. "I understand your situation, Shay, but if I don't ask, I will never forgive myself."

"Ask?" The word caught on her dry lips.

With a wave of his arm, he invited her into his dimly lit room. The lights were dim and a candle flickered in the darkness next to a bottle of wine and two glasses. He shut the door behind them.

"I'm not asking for promises." John spoke against her scalp, his solid chest pressed against her shoulder. As he brushed the hair from her shoulder, his hot breath tickled her ear. "I'm asking for a weekend."

The tips of her breasts pulled taut as his arms closed around her from behind and he pressed his lips to a receptive dip in her neck.

"The weekend?" She trembled as his mouth wandered across her jaw.

He nodded, gathering the mass of hair at her nape, nibbling on a sensitive spot behind her ear, nuzzling into her temple. His thighs bracketed her hips, the feeling of his muscles maddening. She didn't mean to compare, but couldn't help notice the difference between John and Mat. John was bold and adventurous. Mat referred to himself as an ordinary missionary man. There wasn't one ordinary quality about John Mathews.

"But everyone knows my situation." She found herself insanely distracting by minty scent of his breath. "Our families."

"This is between you and I, they don't need to know. Yet." He slowly spun her to face him. He pulled her close. "I understand your situation and I'm not trying to complicate things for you."

She wobbled on her tiptoes as he anchored her to his solid frame.

"I have to know why you make me feel this

way."

Lifting her arms over his broad shoulders, she arched, molding her body to his with only a thin layer of cotton between them. The newness of his flavor and attentive style coiled in her tummy.

John brushed molten kisses of affection over her hair, cheeks and eyelids. He caressed the hollow of her throat, tracing her collarbone with his fingertips. A small moan of pleasure escaped her lips and she closed her eyes as John lowered his mouth to hers.

"Thank you." He murmured cradling her face in his large hands, kissing her mouth gently and tenderly, one lip at a time.

"Thank you?" She asked, feeling his smile broadening beneath her lips.

"For taking that damn ring off." He lifted her right hand, pressing a tender kiss to her knuckles. John squinted flashing her a full smile deepening the soft wrinkles near his eyes. "If I have my way, that ring will never see the light of day again."

Shayla's mouth turned to cotton and she swallowed hard. Something just didn't seem right about the power lying in his words of highhanded assurance. The surety in his tone should've rang like warning bells hanging from the Greek cathedrals, but she found his dominance a complete turn on.

Heat gathered beneath her cami, making it damp. Shayla felt like she might spontaneously combust from the list of aches growing larger with every sweet kiss of his lips. This wasn't simply a first kiss, it was a rich drugging kiss, filling every fiber of her being with desire.

Trembling with an undiscovered fury of passion, she clutched at his neck, opening without barriers, urging him to take more. The heat of their breath mingled as his tongue sank into her mouth, rooting deeper to find her soul. The pleasure of the slow marauding licks of his tongue brought pricks of wetness to the corner of her eyes.

John went still, gently grasping under her jaw with both hands and angling her face upward. Staring into her eyes, he searched intently for her response to their connection. "Stay with me?"

Giving in to temptation, she nodded.

Worry evaporated from his tense arms as they circled around her. He held her securely, learning the curves of her body with an unhurried exploration. The sensation and heat of his hands and mouth felt heavenly and she went weak with need. There would be no holding back with John, not one moment of insecurity or vulnerability. He unshackled the urge to act proper or genteel. She responded with ravenous needs of her own, dipping into his mouth with long, slow indecent licks and kisses. The silky friction and heat turned her kisses greedy as she plunged further, searching for more.

Shayla craved each intimate taste of this man. She molded herself to the terrain of his body, straining her hips upward to discover the hard pressure of his erection. Her fingers clung to the back of his neck for support, and she pushed higher onto her toes. She whimpered into his mouth as sensation built.

John broke from her passionate kiss and laid his chin on top her head, allowing his breathing to slow. A mock whisper tickled her ear. "Maybe we should have a glass of wine."

Heat powered through her limbs. Shayla yanked at the hem of his shirt and he raised his arms, easing out of his shirt. She flushed. "I don't want wine right now, John."

Her palms glided across his fit shoulders. With utmost slowness, she ran her hands over his chest and drum tight stomach. The muted light cast a bronze glow to his skin, deepening every shadow of his physique. Lost in a daze of the magnificence of his body, she trailed kisses and bites over his chest and below. He remained still, tolerating her intimate exploration of his body, each sweet caress more inquisitive than the one before.

A low throaty laugh filled the quiet room. "Are you about done with your inspection?"

She shook her head with a grin, catching her lip between her teeth. She wanted her mouth on him, all of him, every inch. Dropping her hand to his waist, she traced his erection through the denim. He gave a soft grunt and she circled her palm over the bulge.

Using the back of her hand, she traced the satin-smooth skin of his midriff, slipping her fingers into the waist of his jeans. Her thumbs worked to unfasten the button and zipper. Shayla's fingers trembled, reaching in his boxers, exploring the length of him. His abs flexed in response to her hand coasting down the silken heated flesh. His hips pumped forward and he held rigid. Sounds of deep-rooted pleasure reverberated from his throat as he allowed her to stroke him. She felt as if she were in a trance of fascination.

John grabbed her wrist, bringing the tender pale flesh to his lips. A smirk widened across his face at her unbridled haste. "You can have your way with me. I'll give you whatever you want," came a growl of promise.

His voice softened to a murmur, rambling off into a list of things he planned to do to her, words no man had ever said to her, words that would make her blush in the morning light, but right now they turned her on more than she cared to admit.

He stripped her of her top and tossed it to the floor, revealing her petite round breasts. He bent drawing a pink bud into the searing heat of his mouth.

"Oh, God, yes," Her mind blistered. She panted with raw desire.

Moving to the other, John kissed and sucked, circling her nipple with his tongue. He rolled the damp sensitive flesh gently between his finger and thumb until she moaned.

"It's gonna be a long night. But," — he hooked his thumbs through her white lace panties, dropping to his knees and shimmying them to her ankles — "I've wanted to taste you since the moment I sat next to you on the plane. You're lucky I didn't hoist you over my shoulder and drag you into the bathroom caveman style."

"You can drag me wherever you want." Raking her fingers through his thick dark hair, Shayla grasped his skull. Her head listed forward and her eyes closed. He rested his forehead above her trimmed tuft of dark hair. John pulled back and rose to his feet.

Her eyes flew open, pulse raging through her veins. "Wait. I wanted. I like..." she whimpered in protest.

A severe blush flooded over her, embarrassed for objecting.

A throaty laugh accompanied his haughty grin as he guided her backwards one step at a time. Her legs bumped against the mattress. "Oh, you're going to like it. I just want you on your back."

He wedged his knee between her legs, widening her stance as he leaned over her, taking her mouth with another insatiable kiss. Clasping the back of her head, he devoured her mouth with long slippery sweeps of his tongue, the pleasure of it maddening. His fingers threaded through her hair. Tearing his mouth from her lips, he buried them into her neck with a soft moan.

Shayla lowered onto the mound of white, luxurious bedding.

He scooted her to the middle of the bed. The dull light danced across his face. He smiled, descending with a trail of hot kisses down her throat to the sensitive slope of pale skin between her breasts. Her legs fell willingly to the side as he strayed from one breast to the other then below. "You're so beautiful."

John licked into her flesh, torturing her with small tiny flicks of his tongue.

She cried out softly as his breath laid a slick of hot steam over her pulsing clit.

He teased and taunted the engorged skin until she wriggled and panted. He purred with satisfaction, bringing her to a boil with just the tip of his tongue.

She clutched at his head, raising her hips off the bed, wanting more.

John pushed her flat. Grabbing her wrists from the sides of his face, he restrained them at her side. With one precise, deep vertical sweep of his tongue, she moaned out his name. He plunged deeper, nibbling and feasting off her, until her inner muscles began to spiral and clench involuntary.

Shayla wriggled a hand free from his grip, frantically grasping for a pillow. She held it to her face, crying into the fluffy billows as her body spasmed and twitched. She lifted from the bed. His tongue swirled over the explosion of wetness, catching every last twinge of release.

John pressed tender kisses everywhere with acute planning, climbing over the top of her. Brushing his hands along her stained limbs, he allowed her body to go slack.

Quivering with pleasure, she panted hoarsely beneath the pillow.

Resting on his elbow, he pulled back the pillow, peeking at her with a smoldering smile. "Feel good, Shay?"

"Yes." She panted with a nod.

Full-blown arrogance curled at the corners of his lips. "Are you a screamer?"

A fevered rush ached through her trembling body. "Not normally."

Her hands stole at the open waist of his jeans. Strung tight with pleasure, she craved more, tugging at the belt loops with her toes. She needed to feel him inside her. "Take these off," she demanded in a voice sounding unlike her own.

John stood at the edge of the bed and undressed.

Shayla had never seen a man look so damned appealing. Reaching for his wallet, he dug for a condom. Holding the golden foil between his fingers, he warned apologetically, "I only have one." He grinned with a squint. "We'll have to be creative until tomorrow."

She could barely hear anything over the blood rhythm pounding in her ears.

He chuckled tilting his head into her view. "Did you hear me?"

She blinked with a tiny nod. "Creative."

John gently gripped her foot, coasting his hand up her leg and urging her onto her front.

Shayla flinched with a squeal when he playfully bit her cheek. She felt the moist heat coming in ragged breaths as he kissed and nibbled up her spine to her shoulder.

He laid on top her, molding his body to hers, resting his hard-on between her thighs.

"You feel so good." She twisted, reaching around the back of his neck, tugging his mouth to hers. Hungry kisses made her whimper with need.

She couldn't get close enough to him. This man could easily control her with his solid strength and power, yet she had never felt so unbelievably free. Free to be herself. Free to explore a sensual side of her that lay beneath the surface.

Shayla shoved at him until he rolled to his back. Keeping her gaze locked on his, she slid down his taunt abs, one muscle at a time. She grabbed hold of his hard-sprung length, stroked out a slick bead of moisture and lowered her mouth to taste him, briefly, before lifting her head and wiggling her brows.

His body strained and he gripped the linens, letting a few swear words fly.

"We have all night, remember?" she toyed, enjoying his reaction and nodding toward the condom. "I think I have one of those in my necessity bag."

She went down, taking as much as she could into the suction of her mouth.

He groaned within seconds. "Shit. Wait, stop. I can't…"

Candidly, she smiled up at him, circling her tongue around the pulsing head.

A scowl wedged between his brows. He tugged at her, dragging her up his body so they lay eye-to-eye. "You have a necessity bag?"

"Yeah, necessities. Mostly girl stuff. Chapstick, floss, tamp—"

He grabbed her and a laugh of delight whooshed from her lungs as their bodies entwined, tumbling over the bed. John halted over the top of her, fumbling with the foil. He lowered onto his elbows, gently teasing, rubbing and stroking against her clit. Driven by voluptuous jolts of thunder, Shayla wiggled and strained, needing to feel him inside her. Hoarse from heavy breathing, she begged in a voice unlike her own. "Please. Now."

John eased into her with a measured thrust, giving her time to adjust before burying himself inside her. She cradled his jaw, watching as his eyes turned cloudy with pleasure and color burnished high on his cheeks. He plunged deeper and she raised her knees, planting her feet on the mattress, surrounding him with tight lubricous reception. He impaled further, rooting out a tender spot that made her cry out his name.

John buried his face near her ear. "Say it, Shay. Say it again," he murmured, his mouth wandering over her throat.

Excitement climbed higher in her throat as he thrust in perfect stride. She jerked and clawed at the solid muscles on either side of his spine, burying her face in the crook of his arm, calling out his name.

He covered her mouth with his, taking in her cries of sheer bliss. Elevating to his palms, John collected each of her wrists, placing them one at a time above her head, plunging into her with tireless rhythm until her eyes rolled back. John continued, driving the momentum higher and higher. She jerked and spasmed in a kaleidoscope of colors, thrusting upward to greet him. She surrendered, giving into his powerful virility. Shayla shuddered again and again, peaking in multiples. With one last thrust, he quivered and groaned with his own release.

The sound of their raspy pants filled the space between them. Shocked by the slick of tears running from the corner of her eyes, she held him close, nuzzling into his chest.

John nipped at her chin, bushing kisses over her jaw, cheeks and eyelids. Clasping his hand at the side of her neck, he wiped away the wetness with his thumb, peering deep into her eyes. They remained that way for minutes, just staring affectionately at each other, allowing themselves to revel in the tender moment.

A small smiled curved at the corner of his mouth and Shayla smiled back.

"What?" she asked bashfully.

John kissed her nose. "Wonder Woman," he teased, pulling her to her feet, directing her to the shower.

"Superman." She giggled, glancing over her shoulder, letting her gaze drink in his delicious body.

He flipped the switch, illuminating the pristine bathroom with a soft glow. White marble ran its course throughout the bathroom and walk-in shower, bordered with intricate hand-blown blue glass tiles. He pulled on three levers, adjusting the temperature of the showerheads. John nodded, glancing around the pristine bathroom in astonishment. "This place is amazing."

Shayla touched her fingers to the pale grey granite counter, tracing the rim of the white vessel sink. "This is his vacation home. His place in Malibu is even…more incredible."

Curiosity drifted through her mind, imagining what John's place would be like. The throbbing pulse in her neck ached and she wondered if she'd get to see it. She wouldn't allow herself to indulge in too many questions about the future, fearing it'd ruin the moment.

John escorted her into the layers of steam and shut the glass door. He stood behind her, kissing the sensitive dip in her neck. "I don't think anything could be more incredible than this."

Tilting her head back onto his sleek chest, she allowed sheets of cascading hot water to stream over them. Turning into his arms, she draped her wrists over his shoulders, kissing him beneath the rain of water.

His bare form showed off a threatening and well-exercised strength, but he exuded a sense of power that made her feel safe.

He shampooed her hair and washed her body and she did the same to him. His hands roamed over her body, not missing a single spot. She found herself mesmerized by his glistening skin and the curve of each moving muscle.

"How much time do you spend at the gym?" The bemused question slipped out as if she were thinking out loud in awe.

A drone of a chuckle escaped his lungs as he bent, clasping hold of her foot then the other, giving them a thorough scrub. In a macho show of bravado, John flexed posing in several bodybuilding positions. "Not as much as you think. Most of it is genetics, but I do enjoy a good workout."

"Am I a good workout?" She attempted to act flippant and unimpressed at his good-humored show, but her heart slammed so violently as she took in the splendor.

He tugged her into his chest. The length of their bodies molded together as he wriggled back and forth. He playfully washed her body with his. "You're the best workout I've ever had and we just barely made it through warm up."

She could hardly hear his mock whispers over the blood surging through her veins. Subtle aches pulsed, desire building with the slippery friction of their skin.

She twisted, searching for his mouth, drinking in his luscious kisses.

He reached between her thighs and she went still, slumping and resting her cheek on his torso. A veil of steam clouded the air around them. She held onto his flexing bicep, her lip dragging on his shoulder as he stroked her open.

Gently, he slipped his thick fingers deep and held. Her tender soreness turned to pleasure as he started a slow in and out slide. Trembling, she cupped her hand at his nape holding securely. John messaged her tender flesh with his thumb, pushing deeper with an infinite, wicked rhythm, the skilled combination unlike any bliss she'd ever known.

Excitement climbed higher in each of their soft moans, filtering sounds of joyful lust through the mist. Clenching around his fingers, she shuddered against his shoulder, peaking in jolts of delicious ecstasy.

Withdrawing his fingers, he secured her tightly in his embrace. He turned off the water, urgency riddling his tone informing, "We're moving to your room."

In between at least a dozen heat-filled, full-mouth, luscious kisses she could only best describe as the most erotic thing she'd experienced in her life, they managed to quietly relocate to her bedroom without waking anyone.

They sat naked, Indian style on her bed, sharing a bottle of wine. Kissing took on an entirely different role, feeling more like an actual sex act instead of foreplay. They talked and laughed and made love again.

Curling up beside him, happy and sedated in his arms, Shayla drifted off to sleep.

He woke her when the early morning sun filtered into the room.

"Shay," he whispered. Pressing a kiss near her temple, he stroked her arm, his fingers playing across her skin. "I should go. JC wakes up at the crack of dawn every day."

Her brows pulled tight in protest and she snuggled closer, nuzzling deeper into the crook of his arm.

He rolled over on top of her, nibbling on her neck until she giggled. He climbed out of bed and got dressed. "Go back to sleep for a while. I'll make breakfast for everyone in a couple hours."

"You cook?" she asked with a sleepy smile.

"A little." He cracked open the door, peeking into the hallway. John wiggled his eyebrows and came back to her side. He tugged on the sheet, exposing the tight bud of her nipple, bending and drawing it into the warmth of his mouth. "Don't get too excited. Everyone will know how much you *really* like me."

Shayla pushed the sheet to her waist, exposing her other breast. "Hey, don't forget this one."

She giggled in a hush, raking her fingers through his hair as he nibbled on the pale skin.

He pulled back, releasing the delicate skin, pursing his lips to blow on the bud. Heat built in his gaze as her skin tightened, darkening the delicate pink to rosy red.

"I gotta go, Shay, otherwise everyone is gonna know we spent the night together."

John kissed her on the lips and slipped out her bedroom door.

Shayla pulled the silky bedding under her chin and stared at the ceiling. She felt as if she'd been branded, marked as his. No matter how she tried to cover the stains of sheer bliss and guilt, everyone would see it.

CHAPTER EIGHT

Despite all the worry and guilt she should have felt for having sex with John, Shayla couldn't help but enjoy the happy and calmness inside. Her phone blinked green, but it was Carrie Ann reminding her to have fun while in Greece. Mat hadn't called, and somewhere deep down, Shayla knew he wouldn't. After a lengthy conversation with herself, she decided to make the absolute most of the weekend.

Shayla attempted to conceal the *I've just had the most incredible night of my life* look covering her head to toe. She couldn't wipe the smile from her face, or conceal the dark circles from under eyes and chapped skin surrounding her mouth. Sounds of low music and happy voices wandered through the halls of the traditionally quiet house. With each step down the hallway, a new ache or sore muscle reminded her of various positions John arranged her in the night before. Heat rose to her cheeks as she eased her way toward the kitchen, listening for John's voice. Her nerves settled when she found only Tracy and JC.

Wedding talk and a buzz of ceremonial excitement filled the kitchen. The girls moved in unison, making coffee and cutting up fresh fruit, humming and singing, "Going to the chapel and we're gonna get married." Shayla felt like a third wheel for a millisecond, but Tracy and JC quickly added her into the conversation. Their close family dynamics made her feel like a favorite long distance cousin, the relative they hadn't seen for years, but instantly reconnected with like it was yesterday. Besides her uncle, Shayla had only experienced this kind of immediate connection with one other person, Carrie Ann.

Tracy moseyed into the living room, gazing out at the picturesque view. White house's molded into the black cliffs on the adjacent side of the bay, ignited with a hue of tangerine color from the morning sun. Shayla stood at the counter, plunging a tea bag into a boiling cup of water until steam rose with a minty aroma.

JC made a cup of coffee for her sister, and they joined Tracy, stepping out onto the back patio.

The girls' enthusiasm grew with anticipation of the day's wedding.

JC's eyes lit up, glowing the same emerald green as her brothers. "I haven't had my hair and make-up done by someone since I went to my prom."

"I've never had my make-up done by anyone. I'm kind of excited," Tracy admitted.

Warming her cool fingers on the mug, Shayla took a careful sip of hot tea. "Thank goodness for Marco and Rick. I hate doing my own hair."

The sound of the front door opening and closing captured their attention. All three turned to see who was up. John walked through the front door wearing a big smile, dark jeans and a white linen shirt, unbuttoned to the center of his chest.

Tracy and JC exchanged casual good mornings, but Shayla could only stare, her heart pumping in painful beats. Their eyes connected and his grin broadened, raising chill bumps over every inch of her skin. He strolled to the open sliding glass doors, and even though sunglasses hid his gaze from her sight, Shayla felt his fixed stare burning through her like the strike of a match.

Car keys dangled from his fingers. "Morning. It's a beautiful day for a wedding."

He'd turned to Shayla when he said beautiful.

Tracy asked in surprise, "Where have you been so early this morning?"

"The market." His sisters' attention already returned to the gorgeous view hovering beyond the infinity pool. He locked eyes with Shayla. "I needed to pick up a few necessities."

Shayla buried her feverish grin in the rim of her cup and John disappeared into the house, sounds of his footsteps fading down the flagstone hall. Thrilled for their mom to have found love again, Tracy and JC rambled on about the day's events about to unfold.

Though Shayla was overjoyed her uncle had finally found the women of his dreams, the only one thing she could think of was how many minutes she should wait before following John inside. *Two is plenty.* She excused herself without notice.

Making a conscious effort not to run, she paced through the house and down the hall. John's door was open, so she tiptoed inside, shutting it behind her. Ambling out the bathroom door, John smiled. He walked straight to her, wrapping an arm behind the small of her back.

Shayla arched, molding her body to his.

"Do you have any idea how hard it is for me to keep my hands off you?" John raked his strong fingers through her messy morning hair. Cradling and caressing the back of her head, he gazed amorously into her face with a slow, intense burn of hunger.

"Yes, I do." Shayla went slack in his arms as if she'd been drugged, savoring the molded linkage of their bodies combined as one. Draping her arms over his shoulders, she relished in the heat of his neck.

"You are so handsome," Shayla whispered in a quiet breath. Her fingers trembled, studying the indention of his small scar with the pad of her thumb.

He bent, covering her mouth with a slow delicious kiss, sweet enough to make her toes curl. Lifting his head, he pressed soft kisses on her nose and eyelids before staring at her with a grin tucked in the corner of his mouth. "I've been trying to decide what color your eyes are. At first I thought they were blue."

Taking further inspection, he cradled her jaw and twisted her face toward the sunshine casting through his window. "But they also have these long threads of green and dark brown outlined in a honey color. Just beautiful."

She raised her lips and John responded with a quick peck on her lips. Shayla frowned wanting more. She heeded a sensual promise, "You are gonna be in so much trouble later."

"What kind of trouble? Cause if it's the kind of trouble that involves you…well, you might as well throw my ass in jail." He wiggled his brows, nibbling on her neck, causing Shayla to squeal in delight. "But right now, if I don't get into the kitchen in a few minutes my sisters are gonna come looking for me. They already put in orders for my famous banana pancakes."

Shayla dropped her arms from his neck and started for the door.

John caught her around the waist from behind, pulling her in close. His hand traversed the front of her body, fondling and gripping, as his other hand swept the hair from her neck. She tilted her head, exposing her neck. His soft nibbles turned hungry. He tilted his hips, rubbing his erection against the small of her back. He grasped her tighter, murmuring next to the sensitive skin behind her ear. "You make me so hard."

She clutched his forearm, transfixed by the feeling of his muscles moving beneath her fingers. Pushing her hips backward, she twisted her neck, aggressively hunting for his mouth. She felt him smile against the slope of her neck.

Memories of the night before sparked like the flash of fireflies on a hot Kentucky summer night. She only wanted his lips on hers. Shayla slung her arms over his firm shoulders, kissing his mouth with bruising force. Her breath came in hard pants as his mouth moved over hers, the sweet taste almost too good to bear. The slippery friction was so intense her lower stomach muscles clenched and coiled with need.

Knock. Knock. Knock. "Hey, are you gonna make breakfast? Or do you want me to make pancakes?" Tracy issued in more of a warning than a question.

Without making a sound, John backed away from the door, inhaling deep to catch his breath. "Be out in a minute."

"We just woke up Mom and Tom, so everybody's ready."

"Okay. I'll be right there." He stroked down her spine, soothing her trembling body as she rested her cheek on his shoulder. Waiting for Tracy to move away from the door, he whispered, "You okay?"

Unsure of her answer, she remained silent, quivering in his arms as he set her feet on the floor.

Shayla had several boyfriends over the years, but nothing had ever felt this good. John's kisses required full surrender of the moment, leaving her unable to put a coherent sentence together. John peered down, cupping her face in his hands, getting a read on her until she forced her herself to look at him.

"I'm okay," she snickered softly, dazed by her own reaction. "Good lord, you're a good kisser."

She wobbled and he caught her by the elbows. "Do you always kiss like..."

Her words trailed off into a muttering tongue-tied mess as she paced back and forth, wafting her hands through the air exaggeratedly. "I'm surprised you don't have women following behind you like a trail of breadcrumbs. You probably have women lined up around the block for dates. Two blocks. You're just so...yummy."

"I don't have anyone lined up back home." He laughed at her with endearing amusement then said softly, "And you haven't even tasted me...yet."

Her mouth fell open. She was stunned by the heated, somewhat crude, promise and even further surprised by her body's throbbing, wet reaction. Shayla started to say something, but every last one of her brain cells had just been fried. Her brows furrowed together in a tight knit, and her lip twitched. Flustered, she started for the door, stopping to poke him in the chest with a low grumble. "Oh, you are gonna be in so much trouble later."

"You don't know what trouble is." John's arms tightened around her from behind. He growled playfully at the ticklish spot behind her ear. "When this wedding is over, I'm going to take you back to the hotel. Hell, you'll be lucky if you make it to the car."

Relinquishing his hold, John cleared his throat

and opened the door. John patted her on the bottom, gradually guiding her out of his room. "The coast is clear. Go get ready for breakfast."

"Okay."

Pointing his finger at her mid section, he teased in a hushed mocking tone as she hurried toward her room. "But don't you dare sneak off into your room and take care of yourself. You'd better wait for me."

A rush of heat crawled over her from head to toe. She beamed back at him with a smile so big her cheeks hurt as she slipped into her room.

Not even bothering to see if her phone blinked green, she flopped straight back onto her bed. Her feet wagged back and forth, keeping the pace of windshield wipers in a torrential downpour of emotions. She tried to compartmentalize her euphoric high into nice little categories of feelings, but it was impossible. Blissfully happy, calm and content, and turned on would be an understatement.

John's gorgeous good looks were just what lay on the surface. "He's so much more," she whispered aloud. "He's adventurous, and the manliest man I've laid my hands on."

He sported an ego matching many men she knew climbing to the top in the film industry, only he carried it in such an endearing manner. As she stared at the white ceiling, curiosities saturated her thoughts, wondering what he'd be like in his own element.

A vision of him sweaty and dirty after a hard days work popped into her mind. Her lids closed with a slight eye roll as she drummed her fingers on her stomach. She could practically taste the salt on his skin and glimpse the sun-baked, hard-worked muscles.

"Oh, my God and he's so much fun." Her eyes popped open and she jumped to her feet, giggling to herself. She picked up her phone, wondering if she should call Carrie Ann. Staring down at the black device, she shook her head and placed it back on the nightstand. "Don't be ridiculous. He's making breakfast. Get your ass in the kitchen."

Breakfast was in full swing. Shayla opted to keep a safe distance from John and eased onto a barstool at the counter. The man oozed enough sex appeal to cause a traffic jam in a snug fitting white T-shirt and lightweight grey sweat pants. Simply glancing at his long tan feet triggered imploring thoughts. Every time he turned to smile at her, he caught her inspecting his narrow waist and perfectly formed ass.

His muscles flexed and relaxed with each flip of a pancake, causing her to squirm in her seat. John winked at her several times before asking for her to assist him.

Shayla remained glued to the solid wrought iron chair, terrified to get too close to him. But with one tiny pleading glimpse of his brilliant green eyes, she found herself at his side.

His warm smile and spicy male scent traveled along every nerve ending, turning her giddy. Shayla consciously struggled to keep her hands off him. He didn't make it easy and took far too much pleasure in torturing her. He purposely touched her with light, sensual brushes of his hands. He nonchalantly snuggled close to her ear with heated instructions, even going as far as nipple grazing her three times. Her insides felt like an out of control wildfire, burning so hot, her face felt sunburned.

John playfully savored her anguish, secretly torturing her throughout the entire morning meal in front of their families. Everyone vanished when he offered to clean up, leaving just the two of them in the kitchen. Standing at the sink, getting ready to wash the last dish, he dipped his finger in the sauté pan of warm homemade blueberry topping, offering it to her. Shayla wrapped her tongue around his finger, drawing it deep into her mouth and massaging it with her tongue. His humor faded. John's jaw fell slack and his lips parted with the slightest hint of a moan.

She released his finger, nodding at the last bit of sweet syrup, indicating one more lick. She bit back a sultry grin, watching color rise in his tan cheeks. "Shame to waste it."

He gathered the remaining syrup on his finger and watched intently as she took it into her mouth. "Oh, fuck," he murmured in a guttural strained voice.

The doorbell rang, breaking his daze.

"Oh, fuck is right," Shayla warned coyly. She wasn't sure, but swore she heard his breath hitch.

In that moment, everything changed. His eyes filled with seriousness, pulling the gravity in around them. The morning had been so full of mischievousness, playing off their secrecy, but nothing was funny now. Her feet felt like concrete, polarized by his keen stare. John tucked a loose strand of hair behind her ear, lazily massaging the strands between his fingers.

Neither moved, gazing into the other's face.

His brows creased and he tilted his head slightly. Time crept by with utter slowness. Her heart beat wildly, pulsing frantically in her forearms and neck. Her nose stung and her vision blurred through a slick of tears. Tentatively, he reached for her hand, bringing the heel of her palm to his chest.

John pulled her into his arms, but stepped back when the commotion from the living room spilled into the kitchen, breaking the significance of the moment.

"What is this? Rocky's making breakfast and doing the dishes?" came a rough bark of laughter echoing through the kitchen. Benny Levi strolled towards John with a glint of sarcasm in his eyes. His lip curled in a smile as he grasped John's shoulder in a firm welcome. Benny was average height with dirty-blonde hair, a square jaw and cocky smile that drove fans straight to the box office. Almost every woman Shayla knew found him irresistible, including his wife.

John tore his gaze from Shayla, fighting to keep his expression neutral. He rolled his eyes. He dried his hand on a dishtowel, gripping Benny's hand in a vise hold. "Great. Here we go. I'm never gonna hear the end of this shit, am I?"

"Nope!" Lisa Levi declared, throwing her clenched fists in the air with a one two punch. She jabbed John in the arm with a wink, sauntering toward Shayla. She kissed Shayla on one check then the other. "Hello, sweetheart. Be careful hanging around this guy. He's bound to get you in trouble."

Shayla embraced Lisa, surveying John's bright red face from over Lisa's shoulder. She managed to choke feebly, shooting him a timorous grin. "Nah, he's not that bad. I can handle him."

Benny and Lisa Levi were Tommy's closest friends for more than twenty years. Having been happily married for over fifteen years, the Levi's led the pack when it came to the Hollywood "It" couples. Each Levi was famous in the film industry, but together they became legendary. They survived years of harassment in the media and paparazzi, focusing their attention on their family. Benny and Lisa went to great lengths to keep their two children Tommy, age twelve, and Kim, age six, out of the tabloids.

"John, it's so nice to see you again. And it couldn't be under any better circumstances." Lisa turned her attention and innate charm to John. In true Italian tradition, she clutched his jaw in her hands while pressing kisses to each cheek. Her hands fell to rest on his shoulders. "Beats the hell out the last time we met. Oh wait a minute…did I just say that?" Lisa covered her mouth with one hand, ribbing on the jeering even further. "Oh! That's right you were beating the hell out of Tommy the last time we met."

Shayla burst out laughing, hugging Benny and exchanging hellos. She wasn't sure which she found more amusing, Lisa's teasing John or the fact his face verged on a near shade of purple having Lisa Levi just kiss his cheeks. Lisa was one of the most beautiful women Shayla knew and most men she knew grew up with posters of Lisa on their walls when they were in high school. Lisa started her career with a bad-girl persona that softened over time, turning into a well-respected artist and humanitarian.

"Ha ha ha! Very funny. It is a wonderful day," he smirked. John's attention turned to Benny, who wandered toward the backyard searching for Tom. Seeing an opportunity for escape, John quickly followed.

"I thought I heard your voice!" Tess beamed. "Thank you for coming on such short notice."

Lisa held her arms wide. "Are you kidding me? Get over here! I'm so excited for the two of you!"

Emotions of joy trapped in her chest and tears

pooled in her eyes watching Tess and Lisa embrace. They had become instant best friends from the moment they met and acted as if they'd known each other a lifetime instead of a few short months.

"I knew you were the one." Lisa reached for a paper towel, dabbing the corner of her eyes. "Now don't make me ruin my make-up. Get your ass in there and go get ready to marry Tommy. Today, you're going to be a twelve."

Tess stood tall, wiping the tears from her face and nodding with a warm subtle laugh at what seemed to be a private joke. "Today, I am a twelve."

She gave Lisa another squeeze, going over the schedule for what she hoped to be the perfect day. Tess insisted on a small intimate wedding, only needing their most cherished of friends and family by their sides as they exchanged I do's. Tom could've and would've given Tess the wedding of the decade, but that wasn't what she wanted. She didn't need an extravagant   formal ceremony to announce their love. "I just want him. Only him. I don't care about a fancy ceremony or what the rest of the world thinks. This is our day. I have all that's important to me here, right now."

"Screw everyone else." Lisa nodded with a quick jerk of her head. "Do you need any help?"

"No. Marco is helping me."

Tess retreated to her room.

Shayla and Lisa smiled at each other. "Have you ever seen your uncle so damn happy?"

"No. It's nice to see him part of a family. They all seem easy going and...wonderful." She plucked a grape off the vine from the yellow bowl on the counter and tossed it into her mouth.

"I haven't really gotten a chance to chat with

her girls yet, but I met John when he was punching Tommy's lights out." Lisa smiles. "He's a great kid."

"I wouldn't...I'm not sure kid is the right definition." Shayla stammered, a bit of defensiveness in her tone. Heat from her chest climbed up her throat. The ghost of John's masculine touch traveled up her torso.

"Twenty-four may not be a kid to you, but it is to me."

"Twenty-four?" Shayla balked, choking on a grape. She coughed and sputtered. "There is no way he's only twenty-four!"

"Well, he was twenty-four. Maybe he's twenty-five now." Lisa scoffed, lifting her shoulders with an indecisive shrug.

A visual memory of provocative moments from the night before hit Shayla like a tidal wave. Her head jerked back and her lip twitched in contrition. Shayla stood tall, straightening her spine. Her mouth opened then snapped shut. Shame washed over her as a few unpleasant slang terms popped into her head. She faltered and folded her arms across her chest, dropping her gape to the floor. "There's no way he's that young."

Lisa's eyes narrowed with suspicion, followed by a very long observant gape, absorbing every ounce of Shayla's demeanor. She watched in silence, analyzing every detail of her reaction.

Shayla felt like she was standing naked, fully exposed, in the middle of the red carpet.

Tommy entered the kitchen, grabbing a glass of water.

Shayla's gape met Lisa's.

"Tommy?" Lisa questioned, drawing her words out ever so slowly keeping an intense fixed stare on

Shayla. "How old is John?"

Shayla turned away, yanking the refrigerator door open. Standing at the open door trapped in her own ignominy, she pretended to rummage for anything within the reach of her trembling fingers while trying to get a grip on the panic running wild in her head.

"He's twenty-four." Tommy leaned against the counter, joining in the conversation.

"Are you talking about me?" John's rich voice filled with mischievousness, but there was an added hopefulness floating in his tone.

Shayla didn't dare turn around. The scorch of heat coloring her face burned so hot, not even the cool air from the fridge helped.

"Shayla and I were trying to figure out how old you are," Lisa chimed in so sweetly and endearing that no man would know she was fishing for answers.

"I wasn't...we were just talking...Lisa said—" Shayla pulled open a cooler drawer, unconsciously examining the freshness of an apple with a flick of her finger. She felt his presence by her side, stealing the words right out of her mouth. Her skin turned damp at her nape and chest. Having nowhere else to hide, she forced herself to meet his gaze. "I just thought you were...you seem older than twenty-four."

"Nope, twenty-four." A haughty grin the size of the Grand Canyon covered his gorgeous face. John reached across the front of her to grab a bottle of water, slyly grazing the delicate peak of her nipple. "How old are you, Shay?"

The sweetness in his voice sent spasms rippling through her muscles still tender from the night before. Part of her was completely mortified over their age difference, and the other part wanted to tackle him to the floor. "Thirty."

"Really?" He played it off casually, stretching in front of her again, offering waters to Tom and Lisa. He smelled so damn delicious her thoughts fractured, leaving her unable to utter one syllable.

"Are you still hungry?" he added, saving her from a loss of words. His voice remained casual and sedated, but the lust in his eyes gave another meaning. John took a long guzzle of water and set it on the counter. Propping his hip against the granite, he scrubbed his fingers through his rumpled morning hair. His flexing bicep stretched the fabric of his white tee, capturing her undivided attention.

Shayla's gaze wandered over each contracting muscle, craving connection. She scowled in disgust, mortified by her own lust. Closing the refrigerator door, she found Lisa and Tommy glaring straight at her, both wearing confused expressions. *Shit!*

Tommy and Lisa faced each other with curious insight, and then stared straight back at her with arrogant smirks.

"I gotta get ready," she grumbled, leaving the kitchen and their bright stares of speculation. Walking briskly down the hall, she ignored the echo of footsteps coming from behind, willing them away.

"Hey. Wait up," Lisa called in quiet manner.

Shayla refused to turn.

"Shayla Maria Clemmins!"

Shayla glanced over her shoulder, but continued to her room. "What's up?"

Lisa caught up by the time she stepped inside. She waved her finger in front of Shayla in the design of an S. "You tell me! What the hell is going on?"

"Nothing." She withdrew to the closet, mind-lessly straightening of her wardrobe, which merely consisted of two dresses.

"Bullshit!" Lisa threw her hands to her hips, draping her eyes up and down Shayla, throttling her in women's intuition. "You like him."

Shayla's heart thundered. "I didn't know he was twenty-four," she said in an ache of a murmur, burying her face in her palms. "Honestly —"

"Did I miss something?"

She dropped her hands, hesitantly nodding. Her head fell back as she searched the ceiling for an-swers. "Kinda."

"Oh fuck." Lisa paused. "I was just messing with you. Did you sleep with him?"

The ceiling wasn't providing any answers so she tried the floor, shaking her head numbly, morti-fied she hadn't even asked how old John was prior to making love.

"You did? Oh shit." Lisa gripped her thin shoulders. Her perfectly penciled eyebrows rose to a point, astounded by the break in Shayla's squeaky-clean image. "Last night?"

"He looks thirty! Thirty-five!"

"This has nothing to do with his age, honey." Lisa grabbed her shoulders, guiding her in a mother-ly fashion out of the closet to the upholstered chair beside the bed. "Sit down."

She plopped back into the blue chair, folding her sweaty palms in her lap.

"Last I heard, Mat asked you to marry him in front of his whole family. By the way, I personally think that was a little messed up. It's like political peer pressure. Did you turn him down? Tom said you hadn't given him an answer."

Shayla opened her mouth and the entire story gushed out. The proposal, his family, her mixed feelings. "When Mat and I first started dating I thought I was the luckiest woman in the world. How could a man like him even be interested in me? I mean, for a man like him, who comes from such a predominate family, and my family, I just—"

"Stop right there! Don't say another damn word! It doesn't matter where you come from, Shayla Marie Clemmins. You are an amazing woman. Just because you weren't given everything on a silver spoon—"

"Could you please stop calling me by my full name? It makes me feel even more guilty."

A quiet wrapping on the door captured both their attentions.

Lisa grinned so full it bordered on obnoxious. "I wonder who that is?"

"Shut up." Shayla held her finger to her lip, rising out of her chair. She stared at the door. "Shit. I had no idea he was that young. Now what am I gonna do?"

Lisa raked another full examination over Shayla. "Judging by the shade of purple you are turning, I'm guessing he'll *do* just fine!"

Knock. Knock. Knock.

"Shhh." Shayla ushered Lisa toward the door.

Lisa kissed her on the cheek. "The good news is, Shayla honey, I adore him and he is quite a man no matter what his age."

"And the bad news?"

"I'm just going out on a limb here, but I'm guessing you also don't know he still lives at home."

"No fucking way?"

"Way." She reached for the handle. "Good luck.

Oh, and I won't say anything." She opened the door, taking one look at John's patiently waiting form. She held up her finger, informing him to wait a minute and shut the door right in his face. "Honey, for what it's worth, I'm a few years older than Benny. And that John is one hell of a man. I like him."

"Thanks," Shayla grumbled, pulling on the handle.

Lisa clapped her hands together quickly and folded her fingers around each other. "Good luck," she wished John with encouragement.

John ventured into her bedroom without hesitation, closing the door firmly behind him.

Shayla turned toward the bathroom, but he snatched her by the wrist so she should look at him.

"I need to get ready for the wedding," she sputtered smugly. Pulled by a multitude of emotions, she wiggled out of his grip and folded her arms over her chest. "Why didn't you tell me you're twenty-four? And don't pretend you don't know I'm thirty."

"What did you want me to say? *Hi. I'm John Mathews. I'm twenty-four.* It's not an AA meeting. And I assumed you were a little older than me. So what?"

She turned and glared at him. "So what?"

"Yeah, so what?" A smile threatened to curl on the corner of his mouth. "You don't hear me complaining that you're six years older than me."

She stopped, gasping as she spun to glare at him.

A full blown teasing smile covered his gorgeous face as he raised his hands in a surrendering fashion. "Kidding. I'm only kidding, Shay."

He reached for her, but she swatted at his hand. "You just seem so much older. You, you even have grey hair." She ran her fingers through the few silver hairs near his temple.

"Premature. Runs in my family." She held still, allowing him to wrap his arms around her. "See what you have to look forward to in ten more years?"

Shayla pulled back, searching his face. He wore the unblinking gaze of a hawk ready to swoop in on its prey. She swallowed hard, trying to disregard the charm and certainty in his voice. "John, I can't—"

He pressed his lips, soft and warm, to hers, quieting her caution. "You said the weekend. I don't need to convince you."

His mouth wandered over her jaw to her ear. John dropped his chin to the top of her head, covering her heart with the palm of his hand. "Does he make you feel like this?"

She stiffened and pushed at him, but he grabbed her hand and held it to his chest. The hammering of his heart pounded beneath her trembling hand.

"Mat Huntston is not the right guy for you and you know it. When's the last time you had fun, Shayla? Hmm? Hell, when's the last time you even had sex with him?"

"That is none of your business," she grumbled pushing hard at his chest. "Mat's not a bad man. You don't know him."

"He's fueled by the political ambition of his family."

"You're a fine one to talk." She marched into the bathroom. Trying to get away from him, she turned on the shower, thinking he'd leave.

John sighed heavily, reigning in his anger and criticism. He cinched the hem of her shirt and lifted it over her head.

Shayla folded her arms, covering her bare breasts.

"I've already seen them," he snickered in a hushed voice, unfolding her arms and stripping her of her yoga pants. He sat on a stool, tugging her in between his thighs, sending her pulse into double time. "You're the most beautiful woman I've ever laid eyes on. Please don't cover up."

"Do you really..." Her voice broke as he laid a trail of kisses down her stomach. She clasped his skull, running her fingers through his rich dark hair. "Do you really still live at home?"

He looked up at her with a narrow stare. "Yes. I live at home."

She began to pull away, but he gripped her wrists, securing them beside her bare hips. A deep, painful frown wedged between his brows.

"It's not what you think, Shayla. I was in the process of buying a house when my dad died."

The steamy air turned thick with sentiments of loss and sorrow. "Oh. I didn't mean to misjudge—" she said in the ache of a sympathetic whisper.

"I had on offer in on a house and had to back out of the deal. Tracy was going to college in Colorado, she moved back home and enrolled in UNLV so she could help JC and I take care of my mom."

His voice was low and raspy, holding back raw wounds from the death of his father. Shayla got the impression John was letting her inside a small vacant corner of his heart, rarely exposed to anyone if even himself. Embarrassment crawled across her naked shoulders and skittered up her neck.

"I'm not sure if you know this, but my mom was a complete mess after my dad died. She barely got out of bed for eight months. My parents were married for twenty-five years and they had a deep passionate love that...that was unlike anything I've seen. She was absolutely lost when he died. We were all grieving, but damn, she took it so hard. For a while we thought she wasn't gonna make it."

Shayla shook her head, sniffing back tears. She unbound her wrists from his tense fingers and sat on his thigh. Drawing her arm behind his shoulders, she caressed the tension in his neck. "I knew your father died of a heart attack and Tom mentioned they had a great love. Whenever Tommy talks about it, I can tell he has a certain...admiration for your mom and dad's marriage. I know that sounds strange considering he loves her so much, but I think he truly respects the love your parents shared."

"Tom and I talked about it over Thanksgiving." John nodded. A small chuckle rumbled through the humid air. "Did you know he asked me for her hand in marriage?"

She shook her head, pressing a kiss near the corner of his eye, catching the salty wetness streaming down with her lips. "I'm sorry. It's just the whole age thing—"

John lifted her from his lap and rose to his feet, sending a white cloud of steam dancing through the air with his movement. He held out his hand. "Hi, I'm John Mathews. I'm twenty-four, I live in my mom's house, by myself the majority of the time, I make damn good money, I'm hardworking, adventurous, and a bit of a hothead."

"And sexy as hell," Shayla added quietly out the side of her mouth while shaking his hand. Clearing her throat, she attempted to keep a straight face, completely nude, reintroducing herself. "Hi, I'm

Shayla. I'm thirty, I come from a seriously fucked up family, I live by myself," — she pulled a full, encouraging grin from John — "I own my own home, with a little help from my uncle, I love to surf and I'll try just about anything."

"Anything?" His eyes opened wide, clouding with filthy insinuations. A misty veil created droplets on the crest of his cheeks. "Oh, and let's not forget…in a matter of hours we're going to be related by marriage."

John cradled her hand, bringing it to his wet lips. He managed to extract every last bit of apprehension from her body when he tore his lips from her hand.

"We are a pair." Her quiet voice rose above the stream of water. "And I should warn you, I'm in a bit of a relationship pickle."

"You are right about both those things. We are a pair and I've got a remedy for your relationship pickle." He added another heated promise, nodding toward the shower. "You need some help? I could wash your hair, shave your legs, relieve a little tension?"

Shayla giggled, shaking her head. She tossed him a rueful smile, stepping into the walk-in shower built for two, alone.

CHAPTER NINE

The wedding party gathered at the dock an hour before sunset. Two boats waited to ferry them over to a small island for the ceremony. Tommy and Tess gathered beside a small boat painted in customary vibrant Greek colors. Marco and Rick fussed over Tess with last minute touches to her hair and makeup. Not that she needed any primping. Tess looked breathtaking in a creamy white strapless dress that accentuated her curves, and Tommy looked dashing in all black.

Benny, Lisa and their two children, as well as the priest and the photographer, gradually made their way toward the small ferry arranged to transport guests.

Shayla, Tracy and JC gathered at the sidewalk near the dock.

"I really can't believe this is happening." JC rubbed her palms together as if she were rolling a stick in her hand to start a fire, her youthful exuberance unmatchable and undeniable.

"I'm not sure which I find more unbelievable." Blissful enthusiasm replaced Tracy's typically subdued personality. "The fact our mother is marrying *The Tom Clemmins,* or the fact she is just so ridiculously happy. I never thought I'd *ever* see her this happy again."

"You? Tommy's never acted like this in his life. Ever!" Shayla beamed, reaching out to squeeze Tracy's hand.

"Today marks the start of new beginnings," John stated, sending a meaningful glance toward Shayla when he joined the conversation.

Half the comments he made throughout the day construed two different meanings. Each time Shayla flushed from a quiver of a tickle climbing up her neck. What she had first considered arrogance turned to outright magnetic charm. The more he spoke, the more she hung on every sentence coming from his rich voice.

John dazzled her with an imploring smile, lazily straightening a twist in the thin strap of her heather grey dress. His hand paused on the small of her back for an excruciating amount of time, making Shayla want to ease into the muscular contours of his body.

Demurely, she pressed her lips together, blotting her sheer pink lip-gloss. Her gaze inadvertently focused on his black shirt unbuttoned to the hollow of his throat. Unable to help herself, Shayla adjusted his already perfect collar, indulging in the brief contact with his warm, smooth skin.

Shayla noticed a coy smile exchanged between Tracy and JC. All afternoon she observed his sisters taking notice of the attention he casually showered her with. Shayla and John had gravitated toward each other all day. He complimented every item adorning her body. When he admired her stunning grey dress, mentioning how it made her eyes turn the most beautiful shade of blue he'd ever seen, JC mock gagged with a mordant eye roll, muttering, "Get a room."

The moment his sister was out of sight, John nibbled on her ear. "I intend to."

The afternoon sun dipped lower toward the horizon, igniting every nook and crevasse along the shore with dramatic shadows and shading. As they waited at the dock, a man standing alone in the distance caught her attention.

She couldn't get a full view of him because he hid around the corner, resting his shoulder against the side of a stark white building. He lifted his camera, scanning over the sea. The camera wasn't big enough to be a paparazzi's, but the lens aimed straight at her.

Her stomach fluttered apprehensively. The stranger lowered the lens and ducked further behind the wall.

Shayla's eyes narrowed in speculation. "I'll be right back."

She trotted up a set of worn concrete stairs, heals clicking on the light grey stone as she marched down the sidewalk. Her instincts on high alert, she quickened her pace as she passed several local fishermen enthralled in a serious game of checkers. As she moved forward, the man's khaki pants and tailored white shirt became visible at the corner of the building.

"Excuse me." Shayla pointed at his camera.

The man startled at the volume of her voice, gripping his camera. "*Moi? Comment est ce que je peux vous aider.*"

His French surprised her. She would've guessed him to be an American. "What are you photographing?"

"*Photos? Oui. La belle mer.*"

"Who are you?" Shayla held out her hand,

wanting to see the camera.

He shirked away from her demands, frowning uneasily. Peering beyond her shoulder, the man's eyes widened and he staggered two steps back. His face drained of color, turning ashen right before her eyes.

"What's the problem?" John's voice boomed, echoing down the narrow passageway between storefronts.

The man shrugged innocently, his eyes drawn to John's massive set of shoulders. He waved his hands between Shayla and his camera. He rambled on in French.

Shayla glanced at John, shaking her head. "This doesn't feel right. I know he was aiming that camera at me. I just need to make sure he isn't taking pictures."

John pointed toward the camera. His chest expanded as he stood tall, looking powerful and intimidating. "We need to see your camera, bud."

"I don't need you to scare him, John. I can handle this. I'll be right there."

John made a scoffing sound. "I don't think so."

The man's face soured. A glow of fear mixed with annoyance as his casual stance turned rigid. He squared his shoulders in a defensive manner, but opted to take a sulking step back from John. "*Va te faire foutre.*"

Neither John nor Shayla needed a translator to recognize the term *fuck off*.

"Oh, shit," slipped out of her mouth. Urgent to get John out of the situation before it turned heated, she tugged on his elbow, but his feet wouldn't budge.

Shrugging off her loose grip, John shot him a

warning glare. He stretched out his hand, a slight ripple of muscle visible through his black dress shirt warning of his strength. "You. Can't. Take. Pictures. Of. Us."

Shayla kept her voice steady, turning to John with wide eyes. "I don't think he's gonna understand you just because you slow it down and say it louder with a French slang."

"Trust me. He gets it," John assured, venturing a step closer.

As John reached for the lens, a flash of red appeared at his side.

Tracy startled all three of them when she elegantly captured John's arm by the wrist. She darted a sweet glance at the tourist before glowering at her brother. "Is there a problem?"

Shayla nodded at his camera. "I need to be sure he isn't taking pictures of —"

"*Bonjour.*" Graciousness oozed from Tracy's mouth with endearing sweetness as she clasped the stranger's hand, dipping her head to say hello. One look at her voluptuous cleavage stole the edge from his annoyed demeanor. "*S'il vous plaît pardonnez mon frère. C'est d'un marriage privé, et vous ne pouvez pas prendre des photos.*"

John nudged her. "What are you saying?"

Tracy smiled pleasantly, gritting through her teeth. "I asked him to forgive my brother's rudeness. He's a buffoon."

John grumbled indignantly and Shayla dropped her grin to the uneven flagstone beneath her feet.

"Je comprends. J'ai pensé qu'il voulait me détrousser." He clutched his camera protectively.

Tracy smiled. "Imagine that John, he thought

you were robbing him." Her sweet exaggerated laugh carried on breeze down the empty corridor. She mockingly rolled her eyes, showing playful annoyance with her brother. "*Puis-je voir?*"

"*Oui.*" He twisted sideways, allowing Tracy to view is pictures, not missing the opportunity to catch another glimpse at such a striking woman.

"*Merci.*"

He cupped Tracy's hand, pressing a brief kiss to her knuckles. "*De rien.*"

"All clear. No pictures." Tracy turned on her heel, marching back to the dock. "Just one scared to death tourist, trying to enjoy the magic of Greece without getting beat up by my brother."

Shayla nodded, offering her apology, and darted right behind Tracy. "I didn't realize you spoke French."

"I speak a little bit of Italian and Spanish too." Out of earshot, she paused, huffing furiously at her brother. "If you get your ass thrown in jail again, especially today during Mom's wedding, she'll never forgive you. Can we just get on the boat before you make a scene or go crazy on another unsuspecting tourist?"

"Me?" he questioned innocently, poking his chest with his thumb.

Tracy shot him a piercing glare before proceeding to the boat without listening to any excuses.

John called out, "Hey, that only happened once and it wasn't really my fault. Besides, *I* wasn't the one going crazy! I was just backing up *her* crazy."

"My crazy?" Shayla gasped, so appalled, she thwacked him on the arm, knocking herself off balance.

He grabbed her around the waist, his face inches from hers.

She thought she saw a white flash of a grin. "Do you think that's funny?"

"You are so adorable when you get pissed." He pulled her tight to his frame, scanning over her face, taking in every nuance.

She opened her mouth to complain, but he gently pressed his finger to her lips.

"You'd better stop right there."

She creased her brows in defiance. "Or what?"

Her lips moved behind his finger, the scent of his minty breath split her thoughts, tempting her to roll her tongue around his finger.

"Or I might kiss you right now."

"Hey, Romeo! The boat's waiting. Let's go!" JC called, breaking their gaze.

John eased her away from the length of his body, keeping his arm at the small her back, grinning as he waved to his sister.

Fifty questions riffled through her head, including the calling card *Romeo*. She leaned a bit closer into his side as they walked. "Have you really been to jail?" she asked.

Shayla's stride slowed to a crawl as she became fascinated by every intimidating, masculine inch of him. Every part of her wanted to know more about him.

"It's a long story."

"We have all night."

"We won't be talking," he whispered into her hair, escorting her across the bridge made of planks onto the ferry. "Maybe on our next date."

A hush of silence and smiles of anticipation filled the small ferry as it skimmed across the flat, calm sea. Tracy came prepared, retrieving a light shawl from her bag.

Shayla sat next to John, trembling from the cool breeze nipping at her cheeks. His arm came around her, tucking her into his solid frame.

JC swapped seats, squeezing between Tracy and John to hide from the chilly spray wiping over the bow of the boat. She wrapped her arms around herself, nudging her brother's shoulder. Her teeth chattered through an imploring smile. "What about me? You got one of those for your sister?"

"Well get in here," John ordered, lifting his other arm, offering shelter.

JC rested her head on his shoulder and he rubbed up and down quickly, creating friction and warmth on both of the girls' bare arms.

Shayla smiled at JC before locking eyes with John.

He winked at her and she cuddled in closer.

"What did you go to jail for?" Shayla asked, gazing out at the small barren island approaching in the glow of the horizon. She indulged in the comfort of his chin resting on top of her head.

"Nothing. It wasn't that big of deal."

"It w—was a big deal." JC's teeth chattered. "He missed Tracy's graduation and screwed up her party c—cause Dad had to bail him out of jail."

John continued the rubbing, shifting in his seat to shield JC from the biting cold spray of water.

Shayla elbowed his rib, wanting to hear complete details of the story.

"I was on my way to Tracy's graduation and I got into an altercation with someone on the side of the road."

"Altercation?" JC scoffed and Shayla leaned forward, peeking at JC with wide eyes. "More like he beat the hell out of the guy."

"He deserved it," Tracy added flatly.

By now her curiosity dripped like drool from the lips of a Saint Bernhard on a summer day, pleading with her eyes for one of them to continue.

"John was two blocks from the Thomas and Mack, that's where our graduations are held, when he pulled off the side of the road to help a woman getting beat up by her boyfriend."

"Pimp!" JC nodded hotly. "Get the story straight, he was her pimp."

"Beat up by her *pimp*. He got thrown in jail for—"

"Soliciting prostitution." JC's deep chuckle reverberated all the way through John's rigid posture to the side of Shayla's thigh.

He quickly clarified. "I was in a hurry, trying to get to Tracy's graduation, so I took a short cut through a seedy part of town. I passed by a convenient store and this guy was screaming at a woman half his size. He slapped the shit out of her so hard she fell to the ground. Before I realized what I was doing, I had the guy on the hood of the car. *Then* the crazy chick started attacking *me*."

Shayla gasped in surprise. "The lady you were trying to help?"

"The pros-ti-tute!" JC bit off one syllable at a time.

"The cops showed up and took all three of us to jail. Fortunately, my dad had a lot of friends." He tugged her closer, his hot breath gusting hard against her cold cheek. "What were you expecting? Bank robber?"

She giggled next to his ear. "Superhero."

Shayla's main priority should have been the

wedding getting ready to ensue, but her thoughts split like the bow slicing through the waves, parting the sea. *How is it possible to feel this magnitude of happiness? This type of family isn't supposed to exist!* Men like John only lived in fairytales and she stopped believing in those when she was seven.

Her nerves were strung tight with sensory overload. Swathed in his warm, woodsy scent and powerful arm, she felt herself yielding to the rush of passion he unlocked inside her.

For several years the ocean provided her with inner solitude, but not even the turquoise water surrounding the boat would settle her anxiety, and this new brand of desire. He sat so close, yet it wasn't nearly close enough. She trembled, not from the biting cold, but from the lust. She wanted to feel his skin on hers, inside of her. Visions of climbing naked onto his lap and kissing him the night before saturated her thoughts. All Shayla could do was stare straight ahead and smile somberly as her heart spurred in frantic beats.

After docking, the girls gathered their bouquets of flowers. Everyone slipped off their shoes, leaving them on the beach. The Levi's daughter, Kim, carried a wicker basket full of rose petals and their son, Tommy, gripped his guitar as they made their way up the sandy path. One by one, they crested the hilltop. However, Shayla found herself hanging back, not wanting to go without John.

Tommy and Tess's boat motored closer to shore. The captain of the ferry handed John a gorgeous bouquet of red roses that he cradled in the crook of his arm like a sleeping baby. He gave her a half-smile. "I've gotta stay and escort my mom up to the pavilion, Shay."

"I know." The words of understanding slipped from her lips, but Shayla's feet remained planted in the white sand. She fiddled with his collar and adjusted the single red rose attached to his black shirt. Soft strums of the guitar in the distance blended with the lapping of waves on the hull of the boat. Her nose twitched as she held back sniffles.

"You okay?" With a sympathetic gaze, John brushed a falling tear from her cheek.

She nodded then frowned with a slight shake of her head. "I don't know what I am right now. I just feel all weird and confused."

She wiped her nose with the tissue she held balled in her hand.

He hooked his finger beneath her chin, raised her gaze.

"It's just...you're so tough, yet sweet and you're so good-looking and your family—" She hesitated, adding in a quiet whisper, "Are you really like this?

She provoked a slight grimace from him, and his eyes tugged into a deep squint. "Yes, baby. I'm real."

No man had ever called her baby, and she was certain she would've found it insulting if they had. But the way he said it launched fireworks through her veins. "I mean honestly? All the time?"

"This is who I am. I sure as hell wouldn't put on an act or pretend to be something I'm not. Not for anyone."

A strange, unfamiliar feeling of satisfaction rippled down her spine. She quivered. Shayla dug her toes in the sand, glancing sideways at the small boat approaching the beach. Feeling the smooth texture of his skin against her face and the warmth of his breath at her ear, she released a small, pleasurable sigh.

"Today is today. We'll worry about tomorrow, tomorrow. Okay?" He placed a branding hot kiss on her neck. "Go on, I'll meet you up there."

Comforted by the mere tone of his voice and his nearness, she gave a slight nod. Clutching the edge of her dress, she trotted up the firmly packed path, calling over her shoulder, "I'll see you up there."

****

The ceremony took place amidst an ancient ruin, made only more breathtaking over time. Scattered rubble surrounded the open limestone pavilion and three massive pillars remained standing at the entrance. The wedding party stood in front of the pillars in a mix of dramatic colors, all standing out against the paleness of the aged marble. The white and black on the bride and groom contrasted with azure bridesmaid dresses and blood-red roses.

Applause erupted as the happy couple engaged in their first kiss as husband and wife. *This is what true love is supposed to feel like.* Overwhelmed by feelings of respect and adoration, Shayla let tears fall to the weathered marble beneath her bare feet. She stood paralyzed, unable to take her eyes off John. When he turned to look at her with a stare mirroring her own, Shayla's heart soared.

The fiery orange sun began to sink into the Aegean Sea as they boarded the ferry back to the mainland. The reception was at a restaurant overlooking the edge of a cliff near the outskirts of the village. The short drive leading up the winding road was filled with warm hearts and subtle smiles.

The orange glow of heaters and tiny white lights strung from tree branches illuminated the cozy outdoor patio. The dreamy vision stopped each of them in their tracks as they walked through the set of open French doors.

"Wow." JC's voice was filled with awe as she sauntered toward the handrail.

The fiery sky turned to dark blue, and all that remained of the sunset were swirls of soft pink hovering over the caldron jutting out of the now-black water. John's eye followed the simplistic lines of architecture overhead. He seemed to be taking mental notes of the construction of the aged pergola. He gripped the beam, checking for sturdiness she assumed.

Shayla giggled at his inquisitiveness.

"What?" His cheeks burnished with color. He pointed at the rough lumber. "There isn't a nail or screw in this structure. This is impressive. It's all done by hand."

Her lip twitched and she pulled it between her teeth. Sweet sensuality filled her tone. "Hmm. All done by hand. That is *very* impressive."

Her hand immediately flew to her mouth, covering her modest laugh.

Caught off guard by her boldness, John smiled, exposing a set of dimples she hadn't noticed. He reached for her, but she dodged behind the beam, evading his grasp. "There isn't gonna be anything getting done *by hand* tonight."

She let out a squeak when he grabbed her by the arm, drawing her to his chest. A throaty hiss escaped his lungs and a gleam of desire sparkled in the squint of his eyes. John bent to kiss her.

"Beautiful!" Lisa exclaimed with a dreamy sigh. She flashed an exquisite white smile as she sauntered by.

Benny followed right behind her, clearing his

throat and tossing them an all-knowing, smartass grin.

Groups of candles and red roses adorned tables dressed in crisp white linens. Busy waiters served glasses of champagne to everyone standing at the cliff's edge taking in the breathtaking view. Greek music announced the arrival of the bride and groom, and cheers erupted throughout the restaurant and patio.

Dinner was delectable, and as the celebration grew louder, Tommy and Tess gravitated to the dance floor. Old-world atmosphere and the distinct hum of elation filled the evening. When the Greek wedding dance began to play, locals filtered outside to partake in the event, including two of the Greek gods from cliff diving the day before. As more and more local families joined in the fun, Shayla stayed on alert for any unsuspected videoing or picture taking. However, most of the locals had gotten to know Tommy over the years and respected his privacy.

She made her way to the bar and pulled JC off to one side. "Did you invite those guys?"

"No," she assured, holding out her little finger. "Pinky swear! I didn't *invite* them. I might've *manifested* them. Honestly, they saw the party from two blocks away, but I have been visualizing dancing with him all day. Can they stay? Please? I promise they won't take any pictures! I need somebody to dance with."

"Good Lord, I can't believe I'm gonna say this, but okay."

JC threw her arms around Shayla's neck. "Oh, thank you, thank you, thank you! You're the best!"

"Yeah, yeah, yeah, but I want their phones."

The strong fragrance of their cologne seized her

breath as they approached the bar. Neither of the men made a complaint and gladly relinquished their phones. The taller of the two men, who'd given his number to JC at the beach, slung his arm through hers. They headed for the dance floor before the other handsome young man could dig his phone out of his pocket.

"Would you like to dance?" he asked in a brogue accent, cupping Shayla's hand in his as he lay the cell in her palm.

John's heavy hand curled around the tip of her shoulder. "She's dancing with me."

Shayla jumped at the pugnacious sound of his voice. Twisting her neck, she turned to see John and Tracy standing beside her. His stood slack, but looked dark and threatening with a deep scowl notched between his brows.

"Maybe later," the young Greek offered politely, lifting the back of her hand toward his lips.

In one swift movement, John pulled her hand right out from under the guy's lips and gathered her into a one-armed embrace. "I don't think so, bud. She's with me tonight."

A distinct warning lay within his words, and John's green eyes grew murky with the squint of his thick ebony lashes.

John hastily swept her away from the bar.

Tracy's eyes widened in shock, mirroring Shayla's as she passed by.

Shayla carefully tossed the cell phones on the head table. Her fingers drummed lightly on her hips. "He was simply asking me to dance. You didn't have to scare him."

Taking hold of her wrist, he escorted her to the floor. "Bullshit. If I weren't here, guys would be lined up to dance with you like an old-fashioned kissing booth at the county fair," he grumbled flatly, hauling her close.

She couldn't help but chuckle. "An old fashioned kissing booth."

He loosened his hold, but his face held rigid. His heart pulsed rapidly beneath her cheek. John dropped both hands to her hips and she automatically draped her hands over the top of his shoulders.

Her fingers stroked and played with the hair at his nape. "I was going to say no."

Neither spoke, cloaked in the heavy bruised air. Shayla knew he had something on his mind and she waited patiently for the tension to slip from his hold. She eased into his solid frame, allowing him to guide her around the room. Their bodies moved as one as John led her effortlessly around the floor with confidence and fluidity.

He sighed, giving a slight shake of his head. "This has nothing to do with him."

Flickering candlelight cast shadows on the hollow of his throat, his bronze skin delectable. She traced the dip between his collarbones with the tip of her finger. "Today is today, remember?"

The flat of her palm stole to the inside of his open collar shirt; her icy fingers relished the warmth of his smooth skin.

His eyes grew dark and serious. He clutched her hand up to his chest and nuzzled closer into the sensitive spot on her neck. "But I want tomorrow. I...I...I don't even know what to say because no matter how I say it, it's gonna make me sound crazy."

Caught off guard by the confusion muddling his voice, she wobbled a bit, but he held her secure, offering a sense of safety she'd never felt. "I like crazy," she whispered playfully.

A small reverberation of laughter rumbled in his chest. He eased her fully into his arms when a country ballad, *Must Be Doing Somethin Right*, by Billy Currington played. Her eyes drifted shut. She was soon engulfed in the warmth of his breath near her temple as he sang along quietly in her ear.

His rich, seductive voice made her skin come alive, sending sparks zinging through her limbs. John's thighs brushed against hers, skillfully maneuvering her through the small open channels of their family and friends. Everyone and everything seemed to dissolve around them. A fine layer of perspiration blossomed over her skin.

John cradled both sides of her neck with his long thick fingers.

She found the sweet scent of his breath intoxicating and leaned in for a kiss.

John hesitated, glimpsing at their crowded surroundings. His lashes etched a jagged shadow against his cheek. "Are you sure?"

She couldn't hear the music over her heartbeat drumming in her ears. She dropped her hands to his hips, hooking her fingers through his belt loops. Shayla arched forward until their bodies molded perfectly together, giving him all the answer he needed.

Slowly, lazily, John lowered his mouth to hers, never breaking eye contact. His strong fingers coasted over the edge of her neckline with the ease of a feather catching in the wind. He pressed soft kisses filled with utter sweetness to one lip then the other.

She whimpered in delight, catching his lower lip gently between her teeth.

He dragged the kiss to the edge of her eye and beyond to her temple. Suppressed hunger was caged

under the layers of his fine clothing like a thorough-
bred waiting to break out the gate at the Kentucky
Derby. Sounds of need filled his heavy breath, holding back the urgency to take her mouth with ravenous kisses.

Stealing her away from the reception, John led
her through a small iron gate at the cliffs edge. The
moonbeams reflecting off the water below seemed to
follow their every turn, giving illumination to the
narrow concrete path. Her heel skidded on the
smooth round rocks embedded in the concrete, but
he clutched her firmly beneath the ribs. A sense of
security washed over her as she held on to the back
of his hand. *This* man would never let her fall. John
would always be there to protect her.

They hastily made their way to the end of the
short winding trail etched into the natural switchback of the cliff. Luscious anticipation churned in her
as he slowly twirled her around, stalking her with his
lust-filled stare.

John backed her against the smooth pumice
stone wall, still holding warmth from the afternoon
sun. His constrained demeanor lost to desire in a
frantic ravishing of lips, teeth and tongue. "Damn,
woman. You are driving me crazy."

Shayla yielded to his demands, welcoming his
rich, drugging kisses, both shaking, absorbed in ravenous need. His arm fell behind her, gripping tight to
the small of her back. She moaned into his mouth
with a soft murmur, reacting with needs of her own.
Clinging to his neck, she tilted her hips forward, cradling his erection in a rhythmic motion.

Reaching beneath the thin material supporting
her breasts, he pulled, freeing the pale skin from the
confines of her dress. The cool night air worked in

sequence with his fingers, tipping the delicate pink blossoms into tight buds. She arched, lifting her torso and he bent, sucking the tender peaks into his wet, searing mouth. With each tug, the pulsing spot at her center ached and throbbed as if tied together with an invisible string.

Shayla panted and whimpered as he nibbled at her throat. His mouth came to hers, feeding tenderly, giving her long, sinuous licks of his tongue.

John cupped a hand beneath her bottom.

She gasped at the rush of cool air across her bare hips. Her dress gathered at her waist, making her damn near naked under the full moon. She didn't care. Rising to her tippy toes, she rubbed harder against him, tying to extinguish the burning ache right through their layers of clothing. She clung to his shoulders, loving the feel of the strain rippling through the chords of his muscles, grinding against the hard length of him.

For the first time in her life, Shayla *felt* what she wanted. It wasn't a list of descriptions written on a piece of paper. Her heart burst with happiness, excitement and a certain level of unbridled trust that went beyond words in her vocabulary. She couldn't begin to list his goodness on a sheet of paper. There was no judgment, only a feeling of being bound so tightly together, they became one.

"I want to feel you." Her hands frantically yanked at his waistband, trembling to get at his silken skin.

He groaned ruefully. "I didn't come prepared," were the only words she could comprehend between straggling curse words and a few explicit warnings of what she could look forward to in a few short hours.

John held her tight, grinding in rhythm with her hips, encouraging her to ride out the momentum.

"Yeah, but I—" Her voice purred low and hoarse as she reached frenziedly to unzip his pants to take him right there. She was on fire.

"We can't, baby," he reminded with a slight shake of his head. "But I'll take care of you."

Collecting her hands in one of his, John pinned them to the smooth rock above her head. His other hand nudged at her thighs and she automatically complied, widening her stance. Slipping his fingers beneath the elastic of her panties, he clenched his jaw. Exhilaration mounted in his breathing as he watched her face and manipulated the tip of his finger over layers of skin in teasing circles. Each of them released heated exhales of relief as he dipped two fingers into her slick flesh.

She moaned as his fingers pumped, pushing deeper with a small twist. Her inner muscles clenched around the thick intrusion. His fine-tuned rhythm sent spasms rippling in a forward direction.

"Feel good, baby?"

The sweet endearment in his tone each time he called her baby felt like a soft caress drawing her closer to him. She could only nod in response.

Shayla loved the way he looked at her, yearning to give her pleasure. Her slender body curved and she rocked with his rhythm. The scrape of his stubble branded her chin and neck when he devoured her mouth and throat. She twisted, hunting for his lips.

John took her mouth aggressively with keen slick kisses, stimulating her into rhythmic climax. As spasms swelled and tumbled through her, she strained on her toes, lifting her hips, offering more, needing him to extinguish the fervor he ignited inside her. Her body jerked and trembled. "Oh, oh, oh God," she cried out in a quiet whimper.

He covered her mouth, consuming sounds of her pleasure.

Shayla went limp, sagging against him, exhaling a whimper when he withdrew his fingers.

John rolled to the side, propping his back against the rock and hauling her into a one armed embrace.

She stood between his thighs, wantonly sprawled over his front, catching her breath.

Cool air wafted across the back of her exposed legs and layer of humid skin. She stared, watching him bring his fingers to his mouth to indulge in her flavor.

"You taste good. I've never been so damn hard in my life." John stroked her arm and back, settling her trembles, keeping continuous contact with her skin as if he were a masseur finishing the best massage of her life. "I'm sorry, baby. I planned on waiting until later, but I just couldn't help it. I'll make love to you as soon as we get out of here."

"I don't care if it's half-way, all the way, or...or even a quarter of the way. I'll remember this moment for the rest of my life. I've never felt so...so *alive* in all my life." Her voice turned tender as she confessed, "I've never done this outside."

A flash of a grin tucked into the corner of his mouth. Her admission seamed to surprise him. "Ever?"

She tilted her head sideways in coy acknowledgement.

"You'll love the desert." He caressed her arms from shoulder to fingertip with utmost tenderness.

"I'll take you out in the middle of nowhere, bouncing around in my truck near the base of the mountains."

She unbuttoned one button of his shirt then another, pressing kisses to his chest and fingering his dark nipple. So entranced in the sunny vision running though her mind, she allowed herself to drift forward into the future. Intrigued, she asked, "And then what?"

Uncertainty clouded his gaze, as if trying to decide if he should continue. He hesitated, but only briefly. "We'd pack a lunch. I'd teach you all about the desert and take you to see some ancient petroglyphs."

"I make great gourmet sandwiches." Shayla was aware of the fragile ground she walked on to speak of the future. But she couldn't resist, wanting to know what he would be like at home.

"We'd find a little hidden gully and spread out a blanket. I'd turn on some old rock and roll and we would talk and laugh, enjoying each other. We'd stretch out naked in the hot afternoon sun and I'd rub you down with some warm oil. Close your eyes, Shay," he demanded, anticipation lingering in his voice.

She did as he asked, letting her lids fall shut to the night sky.

"Can you imagine doing this in the heat of the day? The sun beating down on us." His delicate voice sent a pleasant shiver down her spine.

A wondrous vision of him lying naked on a blanket in the glow of the afternoon sun sifted through her head. Her lips parted and a heavy exhale rose in her throat. "Ummhmm."

"I'd kiss every. Single. Inch of you. And make love you so sweetly. Or roughly. Hell, I'll make love to you however you want."

"I might have a list." She smiled.

"Then we'd cuddle together watching the second most gorgeous sunset we've ever seen while enjoying a glass of wine."

"And the first?" Her eyes opened.

"Tonight was the first." He held her close, watching her reaction. "And after that, it's Vegas so your options are endless depending on what kind of woman you are. We can lay right there and sleep all night under a blanket made of stars or we could walk the Strip, see a show or even go clubbing all night long."

Leaning fully against him, she couldn't help notice he remained rock hard and rearing to go. Her hand lowered into his slacks, attempting to grip the girth of him in her hand.

His stomach muscles tensed and he gave a long drawn out groan as she stroked down the length of him.

"I'm the kind of woman who would be up for all of the above. And it all sounds quite captivating except for the fact that you've probably done this checklist a dozen times before." Envy pinged in her voice and her insides trembled. *I want that day,* she realized. And she didn't want anyone else basking in the desert sun with him.

"No. You, Shayla, require an entirely new set of checklists."

The sound of heels marching down the path bounced off the lava wall rising above the music coming from the wedding.

"Shit." John edged in front of Shayla, shielding her from oncoming embarrassment.

Shayla yanked her hand from his pants and ad-

justed the top of her dress while John tugged and
straightened the silky fabric around her thighs. She
combed her fingers through her hair, tucking it behind her shoulders. "Am I okay?" she whispered,
motioning toward her hair.

He raised a doubtful eyebrow, adjusting his
hard on with the heel of his hand.

Shayla put her back to the wall, making certain
she remained out of sight, grinning up at him as she
buttoned his shirt.

"Hello?" Tracy called out from around the corner, tipping them off while keeping her distance.
"John? Shayla?"

"Yeah."

"Are you guys descent?"

"We'll be right there." He averted his face, hiding a smile.

Shayla giggled softly, gripping him by the collar and pulling his mouth to hers. She whispered into
his mouth, words and breath caught between
pressed lips, "Tell her we'll be there in ten minutes."

Tracy cleared her throat. "Hello? I'm still here."

"We'll be there in a few minutes." His chest
shook, hiding his laugh as he playfully backed her
up against the bluff. Spanning his arms wide above
her head, John gripped the rock as if he wanted to lift
it above his head and throw it over the edge into the
churning depths of water below. His forehead came
to rest on hers. Both nuzzled each other's face while
smothering their laughter.

"Sorry, Romeo. I have strict instructions from
Benny that I'm not allowed to come back without
you." Tracy cautioned.

John nipped the sensitive curve between Shayla's neck and shoulder. His sweet whisper tickled her

ear. "Let's go, Wonder Woman."

CHAPTER TEN

Laughter and voices ushered along the silent path, growing louder as they neared the reception. *The Way You Look Tonight* played as John courteously held open the gate for Tracy and Shayla.

He tucked Shayla's arm through the bend at his elbow, but Tracy cut them off. She folded her arms across her chest and shirked to one side. A disapproving scowl gathered between her brows as she took a brief survey of the couple from head to toe under the dim lighting.

"Holy shit. What the hell happened to you?"

A tiny muscle near Shayla's mouth twitched. Evading Tracy's scrutiny, she glanced at John for backup. One look at his proud face and the phrase "worked-over-hard" came to mind. Shayla's fingers crept slowly over her face, fixing possible smudges.

Tracy rolled her eyes. She held up her finger, advising Shayla not to budge. After a brisk walk to her table, she returned with Shayla's purse. "I think you're gonna need this."

"Thanks," Shayla muttered appreciatively, wandering off to find the ladies room and a well needed mirror.

After making slight repairs to her disheveled appearance and a light coat of fresh lipstick, Shayla went back to the reception. She stopped beneath the cover of the pergola, catching a glimpse of John dancing with his mother.

Standing in the shadows, she watched them smile and laugh. Shayla couldn't hear what they said, but John's face beamed with pride as they conversed. She felt as if she were intruding on a private moment, but couldn't look away from the love. Warmth climbed up her neck as she witnessed the precious moment.

A moonbeam cast through the slots of aged timber above her head and shined down on her fingers. Shayla held out her hand. Her gaze locked on the white band circling her finger. She licked her thumb and scrubbed at the faint mark left by one week of California sunshine.

"Are you enjoying yourself?"

She jumped, startled by her uncle's deep voice. He draped his arm over her shoulder, rubbing her chilly arm for friction. Both remained quiet, watching the tender scene unfolding in front of them. Shayla nodded. Unable to stop her comparison of this amazing bond taking place before her and the fiasco of Thanksgiving at Mat's home, she peered despondently at her finger again.

"He's a good man."

Shayla glanced sideways at her uncle. She shirked in complete surprise. "I always thought you never cared for Mat."

Tommy gave a raucous scoff. "You're right about that, sweetheart. I don't care for Mat. I was referring to him." He pointed at John.

"Oh." Shayla looked on.

John dipped his mother with ease.

She swallowed hard and added, "He seems

pretty…wonderful. I keep thinking there's no possible way they're really like this all the time. I mean,
seriously. Does a family like this really exist?"

"I thought the same thing when I met Tess."
One of his infamous wry smiles tugged at one side of
his mouth. "I've waited all my life to meet a women
like her. I didn't think she existed. And to tell you the
truth, I was scared to death to meet her kids, but
they're amazing. Thanksgiving was the one of the
best weekends of my life. Missed you," he added.

The sight of her uncle so enamored by a woman
pleased her.

Shayla's gaze drifted to his shoulder and she
dared to ask, "Is John like this all the time? Happy,
fun, charming."

"Yep. And you should add honest, hardworking and protective as hell to your list. And the last
thing you want to do is piss him off." He pointed to
his once blackened eye.

John caught sight of her standing in the darkness and her stomach did a flip-flop like she stood at
the cliff readying herself to leap from the edge.

Shayla tucked her arm around Tommy's waist,
clinging to him like a small child. She rested her head
on the crook of his arm and drew in a heavy breath.
Her uncle took on the role of her father for the most
part, and just the warm spicy scent of him brought a
calmness to her. Every time she caught a whiff of
him, it felt like coming home. "They just seem so perfect."

He gathered her closer, swaying slightly resting his cheek on the top of her head. "Awe, Shay.
We're all just a small adjustment away from making
our lives perfect, but you should never settle for anything or anyone less than the perfect person for you."

"I'm not looking forward to going home."

"You have to do what's best for you, sweet-heart," he said without hesitation. "It's just difficult to say some things out loud and it's even harder for you to hurt someone. I'm guessing that's why you stayed with Mat this long."

The reality of his words sank to the bottom of her stomach like a penny sinking to the bottom of a pool. Her gaze fell to the floor.

"I've kept quiet about Mat *and his family* for a long time, Shayla. I've always tried to help steer you in the right direction while letting you take your own journey."

"I know, but sometimes I still appreciate your advice."

"I planned on talking to you about the whole engagement fiasco while you were here, but you've been…busy. Honestly, you know I've been complete-ly worthless when it comes to relationships, until I met Tess." He stroked her hair. "But if I've learned anything over the course of my life, it's that doing what's best for you isn't always easy."

"I know." She nodded against his chest.

"Life is a journey and everything happens for a reason. That man," — Tommy bent one eyebrow, looking at John in the distance — "has come into your life for a reason. Just like the day you showed up on my doorstep. And just like the numerous days I said goodbye to a nice woman because she never truly touched my heart."

Utterly astonished by the sincerity in his voice, she turned, staring into her uncle's dark eyes that began to redden.

"I can't imagine the amount of perfect timing it took to put Tess in my path. Sometimes, at the precise moment, Fate intercedes."

"The stars aligned that day." Shayla grinned, wiping the slick of tears blurring her vision.

"Only you can decide your path, Shay, but this was supposed to happen. Don't beat yourself up over it."

"You're not mad? You know…your niece, her son."

"Hell no! Is that what you're worried about?"

"A little. The media would—"

"Don't you dare worry about what the media or *anyone* else thinks. You do what's best for you."

By *anyone,* he meant Mrs. Huntston and her political entourage.

Tommy gave her a wide-eyed look of assurance and tapped his finger to the end of her nose as if she were a little girl.

"I love you, Tommy. You know I think of you more like my dad."

"I love you too, but let's not start that conversation. I'll be crying like a baby again." He squeezed her shoulder and nodded toward John leading his mother toward the pergola. "And right now, it appears as if you're wanted on the dance floor."

John never took his eyes off her until he relinquished his mother's hand to Tommy. Shayla immediately reached for John's hand, greeting him with a kiss on his neck. *Moves Like Jagger* started playing and the newlyweds wasted no time making their way back to the floor.

"Let's tear it up," John said, following right behind.

John gained her undivided attention, moving seductively over her body as he danced. He took control, pulling her close, artfully molding his hips to hers. He wore a haughty wide smile, practically laughing out loud at her stunned expression as he lithely rolled his body against hers like a snake.

The heat on her skin climbed, and Shayla felt a prickling sensation bourgeon as he charted every curve of her body. Part of her wanted to run for cover, and the other wanted to melt into him like a hot shower. His rising body temperature heated his fresh, spicy cologne, filling each breath of air with his aroma.

Warily, she dared to take a quick glimpse around the room to see who watched, only to find each couple dancing with the same enthusiasm and confidence. "What did you say you do in Vegas?"

"Don't judge. I only did that part time when I was younger to make extra cash."

Shayla stood paralyzed in a wide-eyed stupor. A flash of his white sardonic smile caught her eye. She grinned over her shoulder as he danced around her. "Should I go get me some dollars?"

"You get it free," he growled, provoking a squeal of delight. Every flexing muscle swayed and bumped against her backside. "I'll teach you some new moves tonight."

"Oh, I think I can manage."

He sauntered to her front side. Glancing down at her sharply, John gripped her hips. "You're in for a long night, baby."

****

Benny and Tracy each gave a touching toast about sentiment and gratitude of newfound love, a love that would last the remainder of their lifetime. The toast was meant for Tommy and Tess, but Shayla and John held to each other silently, listening to every word. Shayla's chest ached and a severe rush of heat climbed up her neck. Her earlobes burned and she held back tears, overcome with a new desire for an endless tomorrow. Shayla yearned for her own happily ever after.

Reflexively, she molded her back against his wide chest, trembling from head to toe, submerged in incredulous feelings of adoration for a man she barely knew.

And damned if he didn't dissect every tremor.

John held her shoulders. His lips searched the sensitive curve on her neck, making a sympathetic sound. "It's okay, baby."

She shook her head, willing away tears that continued to threaten to come again. Words tumbled anxiously from her lips. "Actually, it's not okay. I don't get it. I feel like a gushing bumble of nerves ready to cry at any given moment. I don't know if it's Greece or the wedding or—"

"I'm not feeling myself either, Shay." The raw honesty in his tone simmered her angst. It wasn't Greece or the wedding. John hauled her close and peered over her shoulder, raising his glass of champagne to hers. "But I can tell you this much. In about two or three more songs neither one of us is gonna care. And the only thing you'd better be crying out is my name."

Right on queue, *Maybe I'm Amazed* by Paul McCartney began to play, drawing them to the floor. John sang softly near her temple, his exhalations floating across her cheek. He maneuvered her through the song with finesse. They kissed openly. It started with elusive touches of parted lips, but with each passing chorus the connection held longer and deeper.

JC danced beside them, leaning closer, nudging

her brother, and joining in with the climactic, "'Oooooo.'"

John tossed a luminous smile and an eye roll at his little sister.

Shayla smiled into his shirt, finishing the song with them.

"I'm surprised you know this song." A mock grin tickled the edge of her lips as she made reference to his young age.

"The only class I managed to pass in my first and only semester of college was The History of Rock and Roll."

"You didn't finish college?"

His fingers spread wide on her back, spanning the narrow cage beneath her shoulder blades. She gasped a little as he gripped her firmly to the length of his body. "I'm more of a *hands on* kinda guy."

****

It was late when they arrived at the trendy, five-star hotel. Welcomed with a signature cocktail, Tracy and JC meandered through the lobby, taking in the nature-inspired atmosphere one painting at a time.

John rested an elbow on the counter, mindlessly playing with a lock of Shayla's hair, never taking his eyes off her. She'd previously made reservations for three rooms. When the clerk presented their room cards, he pressed his pointer finger on top of a card, sliding it back to the clerk. "We won't be needing this one."

"Actually, that's my room key." Shayla retrieved card and pushed another toward the clerk. "And it's a suite."

"Of course *you* have a suite."

"Perks of making the reservations. Comes with

the job."

John murmured, nipping her ear, "I'm gonna give you some perks with the job."

Shayla released a shaky laugh. *God, I love his sense of humor!*

His deep chuckle strummed down her spine like caressing fingers as they made their way to the room.

The lights flickered on when the door opened. Crossing the threshold into the romantic sanctuary, Shayla's nerves sizzled like holiday chaser lights. The stark white suite was built with rustic, authentic architecture, harmonizing perfectly with modern elements. She ambled toward the sliding glass door.

Coming up behind her, John grabbed her upper arms. "Come here, you. The only view I'm interested in is you, in just about any position you can dream up."

His thick fingers griped tightly, lifting her shoulders as his mouth descended to her neck. She gasped at his sheer strength and power, and arousal poured over her in a relentless wave. John grazed over the sensitive slope of her neck. He focused his attention there, searching for hidden pleasures, pressing slow, burning kisses to her skin. She sagged against him with a heavy exhale. One hand held her securely, his other wandered over her front, working her into a fevered pitch.

Shayla turned abruptly, grasping his face in her palms. Violent trembles shook her fingers, and she stared up at him breathlessly.

Crushing her lips to his, she panted beneath their lips. "I want you so badly."

John obliged, matching her lustful cravings with hot deep glides of his tongue. His fingers tangled in her mane, clasping firmly to her skull. He kissed her until she was dizzy with need.

The roughness of his hands caught against her bare hips and she groaned into his mouth. He stripped the dress above her head, the weight of her clothing disappearing. Her fingers worked hastily, impeding her effort to unbutton his shirt. Her lips broke away over the rasp of his stubble. "Now. Right now."

"Easy, baby." The pad of his thumb made leisurely circles on the side of her neck, soothing her rush. He pried her fingers away, bringing them to his lips for a kiss, and began to undress.

Pitifully amused by her own desperate need, Shayla held her hands to the side of her head as if holding it from the pain of a migraine. She paced back-and-forth wearing only her black panties. Her high heels snagged a bit on the Berber carpet as she dragged her feet in bemusement. "I've never felt like this before." She spoke the words aloud, but said it to herself. "I feel like I'm on fire."

He came to her, caressing her limbs in a reassuring manner. "Just relax, baby. You okay?"

"You're just so..." Her gaze lowered to the masculine dips and textures of his body, her anxiousness decelerating. "Handsome and manly. I've never been this attracted to anyone."

Shayla timidly reached out, tracing her fingers down the taught bands of muscles. She played with the dark hair on his lower stomach. He was heavily aroused. She gripped him, tenderly fondling his taut skin. She touched him with curious wonder, startled by the new sensation building in her chest. When her gaze lifted, a storm brewed in his eyes, drinking in her body with the same thirst.

He released her and opened his suitcase, digging for protection.

Shayla noticed a *Bare Your Soul Calendar* placed perfectly in the mesh zipper compartment. She peered over his shoulder, reaching around him to grab it. "Hey. Where did you get that?"

"You're not supposed to see that." He shut the suitcase and turned so they faced each other. His brown skin flushed crimson high on his cheeks. "That's mine."

"Where did you find that?" Shayla grilled.

"Somebody, a publicist or someone, sent several to my mom. I saw it on their computer and nabbed it."

"What did you think? Did you like it?" She poked his stomach.

"What did I think?"

"You didn't like the photo?" Her shoulders dropped and she let out a sound of discouragement. Her voice sounded more dejected than she intended.

His finger cut through the air, making a triangle of her private parts. "I think those are mine. That's what I think!"

Uncertain if John was seriously unhappy, she blanched, folding her arms over her breasts.

"That being said, it's the most beautiful picture I've ever seen, but I wanted to break that surfboard in two when I read it was a *man* taking the photo." John unfolded her arms, holding them open to gaze at her body. He eased her into his embrace. He shook his head slowly, guiding her arms around his neck. "No more naked photo shoots."

The heat radiating off his hard-on wedged between her thighs made her squirm. "What? No, you can't tell me —"

He raised a brow, rocking his erection between her thighs, daring her to complain.

"What were you going to say?" He stared straight into her soul. Using skilled accuracy, he maneuvered her panties to the side, pushing further, gliding over her wet flesh. His ridge slipped over her swollen layers, sending a *zing* of pleasure through her. He made short, deliberate thrusts again, pulling a moan from her throat. "That's right, baby. These are mine."

His bravado reached an all-time high as his fingertips circled a breast teasingly.

Her breathing wasn't right, and she couldn't think right either. She clung to his shoulders as all rational thoughts left her brain. At that precise moment, she might've followed him anywhere or done anything he asked. She had fallen prey to his masterful charisma.

"Do you like this?" He nudged again. His question dripped with sincerity, yet his eyes held a naughty, playful grin.

"Honestly, I like everything about you," she panted.

"Tell me you won't pose nude in front of another man again."

He stopped all movement. John's thick fingers spread wide, grasping both ass cheeks. He held her firmly with an imposing stare, both brows bent, waiting for her reply.

Dangling on a pendulum, Shayla was torn between complete irritation and zealous lust. He was pushing her buttons, asking her to make promises she wasn't ready to say aloud. If she said yes, she feared she would lose all rational thought and bury him deep inside without thinking twice about the consequences.

She shimmied off him and snagged the condom from the top of his suitcase. Shayla shoved at his chest, pushing him backward onto lounger at the foot of the bed. She wasn't sure who looked more stunned, her or John.

"Oh, shit. I'm—"

Stifling his apology, she pressed her fingers to his lips, requesting his silence.

Hands skimming over her hips, Shayla slipped her middle fingers into the sides of her panties and dropped them to the floor. Somehow managing to keep a straight face and her nerve, she lifted her leg and placed her high heel on the lounge outside his thigh. She had never been so assertive in her life.

Astonishment washed over his stunned expression as if she had just blown his mind. His breathing labored and his eyes dilated. He let his head list to the side, taking in the full view.

A feeling of power simmered through her as she enjoyed the effect she had on him. Insecurities she'd worn like a sweater all her life were replaced with a calm inner comfort she'd never known.

"It was for charity and a good cause." She wiggled the foil.

John blinked repeatedly, having difficulty removing his gaze from her sexy show of exposure. He swallowed, then glowered. His gaze narrowed to a somber frown. He rested his forehead to the slope between her bare breasts. "*I'm* a good cause, Shay."

Something was happening between them. She could only describe it as energy, a current of magic energy tingling at her core.

"Okay, I won't pose for any man but you," she conceded softly without hesitation, digging her fingers into his dark hair and cradling his head.

They each moved instinctively.

Shayla lifted her other knee, straddling his thighs.

John held her tightly, tugging her onto his lap. He nudged at her opening, breaching the snug barrier.

She braced herself, lacing her fingers at the back of his neck.

He cupped her bottom suspending her, and she took him in slowly, yielding to his impalement.

They stared at each other. She settled lower, giving way to the thick intrusion, engrossed with the sound of his breath coming in rugged groans. Her back arched, and Shayla reached behind her, placing each palm on his knees. Raising her chin to the ceiling, she fluttered her lashes as John filled her with the rest of this lustrous heat. She lost sight of his gaze, as her eyes rolled back into her eyelids.

His hands held her, strong and secure, allowing her to ride him freely. His thigh muscles strained beneath her as he began to thrust, taking all she had to offer, silently demanding more. A pleasured cry rose in her throat and he brought a hand to her front, his thumb circled her clit until she moaned out his name.

"You're not done, baby." His rough voice heeded a sensual warning while his finger worked her into madness.

She couldn't keep quiet, groaning in ecstasy, clenching and pulling at his rigid length.

John's other hand threaded through the damp hair at her nape, gipping the base of her neck, compelling her to meet his intense stare. Another set of spasms tumbled through her. He smiled as if in a trance, watching keenly, bringing her to the pinnacle of an unchartered climax. And when she thought he had finished, he took control of her wilting frame, clutched her by the waist, and planted her feet on the lounge. She wriggled at the fullness.

He licked and ate at her throat, her chest and her breasts. "I want you. Fuck, you feel so good."

His rhythm quickened with need and her body responded, giving it to him, riding him hard until he smothered his moan in her neck with a shudder of release.

Breathless, she buckled, laying her cheek on his shoulder. Her arms curled beneath his, holding to the surface of his back.

John pressed his mouth to her neck.

She felt the curve of his smile against her skin, struggling for air.

John cuddled her close in his lap and she dropped her head, snuggling into the comfortable dip between his shoulder and the prominent bulge of his bicep.

Staring wordlessly into each other's faces, they drank in the tenderness of the moment. A thin layer of perspiration covered them. The sweet fragrance of lust and love, heated by passion, wafted through the air between them.

Her messy hair cascaded to one side and he smiled affectionately, fingering though it, brushing a stray strand from her cheek. Shayla caressed his face with absolute slowness, relishing in the texture. Her finger traced over the small scar on his cheek. "How did you get this?"

He cupped her bottom and rose to his feet, heading for the shower. "It's not near as good a story as what you're expecting."

"What? No jail time?"

"Nope. There was this mountain lion—"

She burst out laughing.

He set her feet on the floor and gave her a grin that made her heart stop. "I played baseball in high school. I was on the mound and took a line drive to the face. If you look real close, you can see the thread marks, but most of them have faded."

He continued with his story, proudly showing off a few other scars as they showered. They talked and kissed, sharing stories. Shayla loved listening to him talk. Even though he'd been raised in Las Vegas, John wore an old school vibe, an old-fashioned goodness, filled with manners and self-reliance.

In a blur of conversation they dried off and climbed in bed. She lay on her side, her head resting in the crook of his arm. The sheer masculinity of his features intrigued her, drawing her in.

John twirled the strands of her sodden hair around his finger, leaving them in a corkscrew curl. A small wondrous smile lit up his face. "You have great hair."

"That is the cheesiest line I've heard from you yet."

"I haven't used *a line* on you yet. With you, everything seems to pour out," he assured, releasing another coil of blonde hair. "It's straight but wavy, it's just so perfect and yet messy."

A slight tremor scratched down her back and her brows puckered. Shayla felt the lobes of ears turning hot.

"Did I say something wrong? That was supposed to be a compliment."

"No, it's not that. It's just...I used to get in trouble for having *messy* hair when I was a little girl."

"Seriously? I bet all little girls have messy hair

at one point or another."

"Not at my house. At my house you got your hair chopped off with a knife." The words tumbled out of her mouth before she had time to add a filter.

He cringed at the idea, pulling her closer and pressing a kiss to the top of her head. "That's horrible. Why would your dad do that?"

"My mother did it. Twice. I used to get high anxiety when I was little, and I would twirl my hair constantly. My house was a war zone. My dad would find any little thing to zero in on and blow up into a huge fight. Instead of sticking up for me, my mom grabbed a chunk of my hair and lobbed it off with a steak knife."

John stiffened.

"I had to wear it that way to school for two weeks before she chopped off the other side. My mother was just trying to save her own hide." She tilted her head in a nod of confirmation. "If she didn't react quickly enough to his crazy outbursts, by the end of the day, he'd spiral into this deranged psychopath and beat the hell out of her. She would've done just about anything to keep the storm from brewing."

"I'm sorry you had to go through that, Shay."

"It actually feels good to talk about. I usually don't because it's so humiliating."

"You don't have anything to be ashamed of, Shayla. You should be proud you had the guts to get out. You don't ever talk to anyone about your past?"

"Other than Tommy and the therapist he made me see for a few years, I've only told my best friend Carrie Ann. She runs the *Bare Your Soul* campaign."

John held her with the infinite tenderness of an injured animal, stroking and caressing her fingers.

"You don't have to hide anything from me. I want to know everything about you. I would never judge you, baby."

Her toes tucked between his calves, and she snuggled closer, kissing his chin, whispering against his neck, "I know. I trust you."

Shayla took comfort in the safety of his arms. She knew he would never ask her to be what he *needed* her to be. This man would be happy letting her exist exactly how she was.

CHAPTER ELEVEN

Exhausted and sedated, Shayla lay tucked beside John as the early sun crept through the sliding glass door of the balcony. She let out a happy sigh, savoring the hard muscled surface of his arm beneath the slant of her jaw. As she stretched, long, subtle aches pricked over every inch of her body. She pressed her smile to his skin and curled into his warm morning scent.

The night had only ended a few short hours before. She'd done things with John Mathews she'd never attempted before, and took mental notes of a few things she wanted to try. Whatever restraints she'd had before dissipated with John. She felt uninhibited and alive in her own skin. He twisted and arranged her in positions she thought were only possible in a Kama sutra. They made love and talked all night long about life, goals, dreams, and places they each hoped to travel. John opened up about his father, Richard, and how his death took a toll on their family. The admiration and respect he held for his father moved Shayla to tears, touched by their bond.

John stretched with a shiver, yawning above her head, pulling her back closer into the mold of his body.

Shayla held to his arm tucked between her

breast, tracing the muscled chords and dark hair. She couldn't touch him enough or bring him close enough. They lay slumbered together in silence until she begrudgingly made her way to the bathroom.

"Hey, baby, your phone is buzzing," John called from the bed.

The hairs on her arms rose to daggers and her stomach eddied like a behemoth wave on the coldest day in January. "Umm. It's okay, just let it ring," she mumbled through a mouth of foaming toothpaste.

John's large frame appeared in the doorway, dark and heated. "It was your fiancé," he bit out snidely, his typical smile turning to stone.

Her heart beat in deep throbbing palpitations, pounding in her ears, filling the awkward silence. The anger and pain washing over him in waves pulled streams of tears from her eyes. She rinsed her mouth, and her hands trembled, wiping the residue from her lips.

"He's not my fiancé." Shayla forced herself to meet his glare before peeling away her blurry gaze. She stared blindly through a slick of tears at the shower. All she could think about was just a few hours ago it was the best shower she'd ever had. The place they retreated in the middle of the night to make love under a veil of steam now seemed sterile.

John stood naked and rigid, his thick fingers creasing white as he held onto the doorjamb.

She feared he might rip it from the wall.

"I'm sorry," she said. Her heart twisted in sweet pain, bursting with words, big words. Sentiment and emotions danced through her heart, climbing high in her throat, wanting to break free in her voice. Words that previously seemed awkward with Mat wanted fly out of her mouth without a second thought. "I...I...think I—"

"Don't," he warned before turning his back as if he were shielding himself from her words. John aggressively shoved his hands through his sleep mused hair, nearly yanking it from the roots. "Don't say things to me...if there's even the slightest chance you might rip them away from me tomorrow."

"But I want to. I feel things I've never felt before." Her mouth was so dry it came out raspy and shredded. Dread chilled in her stomach.

John spun around. He gripped her arms, lowering his face inches from hers. "Don't you dare tell me you love me unless you plan on leaving Greece and coming home with me to Vegas. I'll buy a house tomorrow!"

"I can't do that, John. I have to be fair to him."

His expression sullied as if she'd punched him. He dropped his hands and stepped back, repulsion hanging from his open mouth. "You have to be fair to *him*?"

"I owe him that, John." She tried to touch him, but he pulled further away with every word. He dug into his suitcase and jerked out a pair of jeans, cramming one leg at time into the worn denim, minus the boxers. The sheer masculine sight of him with his zipper undone left her momentarily speechless. "I need to see him in person. I have to take his situation into consideration. I know you don't want to hear it, but I need you to understand."

"Sorry. I can't really wrap my head around his situation." Rage and resentment trampled through his words. The punitive tone of his voice pulled old triggers and she trembled.

"Please don't," she said, her voice barely a whisper.

John stretched a long sleeve t-shirt over his head. His glare turned unhappy with her lagging silence. "Do you understand how I feel? I don't want you to go home to him. I don't want you to kiss him, I don't want you to…to have sex with him while you're off in California trying to tell him goodbye."

She twitched at his crudeness, coloring with shame. "No. I'm not going to—"

"Bullshit!" John slammed the table with a harsh thud and she recoiled, drawing in a sharp gasp. "It's the first thing he's going to do, Shayla. He's gonna welcome you with open arms, kiss you hello and take you to bed. It makes me so fucking angry I could—I could rip him in two."

A quiet sneer scraped from her tight, dry throat as she shook her head. Mat would never greet her that way.

John misunderstood her scoff. Color drained from his face. He wasn't breathing and his eyes turned dark.

She reached for him. "Wait, that's not—"

John backed away, but when she continued toward him, any remaining calmness vanished. He clutched her upper arm securely as if it were a lifeline. "You think this is funny?"

"That is the farthest scenario from the truth. Mat would never greet me that way. You don't know him and *no,* I don't think any of this if funny! I'm not trying to hurt you."

He held his hands out, stiff-arm fashion, a clear gesture of back-off. His face contorted in jealous rage and beads of sweat gathered on his forehead. If it were fifteen degrees cooler outside, steam would've risen off his skin in a cloud when he walked out the door.

****

Shayla got dressed and finished packing, not wanting to wait another minute to get things settled with Mat. She sank to the edge of the bed reading his text, *Hope you're not working too hard. I was looking forward to seeing you tomorrow, but I have a meeting in Washington. I'll be home in a few days.*

She waited twenty minutes before deciding to go look for John. Rounding the corner at the end of the T-shaped hall, Shayla nearly toppled into Tracy and JC. Each held a cup of coffee to go. JC wiped at the hot liquid now dripping down her forearm.

"Have you seen John?" Breathless, Shayla grabbed Tracy for stability.

"No, we just came from the lobby. Was he getting coffee?"

Shayla frowned warily, making her way around them. "Umm, no. He…went for a walk."

The girls raised their brows, cringing and simultaneously saying, "Oh," dragging out the one word syllable.

Shayla felt like a cartoon character slamming on the brakes. "What does that mean?"

"Was he upset?" Tracy asked.

Shayla nodded and JC looped her arm through the bend at her elbow, coaxing her back toward her room. "You should just give him a few minutes. He'll be back."

JC tucked her long, caramel hair behind her ear and patted Shayla's hand. "Was he barefoot?"

Shayla nodded incoherently, gaping over her shoulder, wanting to run down the empty hall toward the lobby.

JC shook her head adamantly. "If he took off *and* he's barefoot, you definitely need to give him his space."

"Seriously?"

Approaching her doorway, Tracy motioned for Shayla to hand over her room card. "It's his way of keeping himself in check. He just needs some time to cool down."

"He's been doing it since he was little." The click of the door unlatching mingled with JC's low understanding laugh. "He'll be back. He has to, he has no shoes."

"He's just like our dad. That's the only way we knew our parents were arguing."

Shayla couldn't wrap her head around the out-rageous idea. "*This* is how he argues?"

****

Sometimes having patience seemed more like a jail sentence than a virtue. They were already late for their flight. Shayla waited an hour and thirteen minutes before John walked through the door. Sitting on the edge of the bed, she clutched her phone. "I don't even have your number. I was worried—"

"We're gonna fix that right now. I already have yours, in case you were wondering." He stood between her thighs, peering down at her. Dark bruising circles highlighted his red eyes. John retrieved her phone and entered his number. She remained quiet, unsure of what to say. "I know what I signed up for when we agreed on the weekend, but I had no idea how I was going to feel about you. I don't like this one bit, but...you go do what you have to do."

"I was expecting him to be there when I get home, but he's going to Washington and won't be back for a few days."

"You spoke with him?" came a growl.

"No, I just read his text."

He tugged her from the bed and into his powerful embrace.

She went slack, nuzzling into his chest, inhaling the salty air lingering with his familiar scent.

"Come home with me. I'm not gonna be myself without you, Shay. You settle me." His low voice purred along her temple in a pleading hush.

Wrapped to his waist, she lifted her chin. He caught her bottom lip between his. "Can't. I have meetings and phone conferences scheduled all day for…I don't know how long. Days? Weeks? It's gonna be crazy. My boss, Tommy Clemmins, just got married."

Her fingers crept up his chest, curling around the back of his neck, encouraging him to deepen the kiss. Slowly, torturously, he relaxed into her mouth, possessing every sensitive spot he now owned.

****

The twelve hour flight felt like it raced by in twelve minutes. The armrest acting as vital separation from John on the flight to Greece was now immediately hidden between the fully reclined leather seats. They both lay on their sides. Shayla snuggled as close as she could get with her arms tucked between them. John caught her hand, kissing each knuckle before taking her mouth in a fierce, insatiable kiss.

Neither spoke much, only low murmurs between dozens of erotic toe-curling kisses and heavy petting that nearly made her climax in her seat. Shayla didn't want to sleep, but eventually dozed off, half-stretched across his lap.

A dim glow illuminated the plane's interior, casting shadows over John's slumbering face. Sleep relaxed the tiny muscles near his eyes, depicting his age more clearly. Unaware of how long she'd slept or where they were in route, Shayla dreaded the fact she was closer to Vegas. Wetness gathered between her cheek and the warm leather. She wiped her face and untangled herself from John, climbing over him carefully so as not to disturb him.

"Where are you going?" he asked, his voice a strand of silk.

She bent, nuzzling his ear. "Be right back."

He locked onto her wrist, blinking to adjust to the darkness. He examined her face, frowning with concern.

She smiled, carefully, and winked, easing out of his grip, hoping her sadness would be masked as fatigue from jet lag.

She escaped into the lavatory and locked the door. Glimpsing her shattered reflection in the mirror, she grabbed a hand towel from the stack and ran it under cold water. She held it to her puffy eyes, praying it would ease her pain.

"Shay?" he whispered at the door, knocking lightly.

She tossed the rag in the sink and opened the door. Unable to muster a smile, she merely stood there.

John maneuvered into the cramped quarters and she backed against the small granite countertop. Taking one look at her, he gave a sympathetic hum.

She folded her arms across her chest. "God. Please stop making that sound. It makes me feel even more pathetic. Seriously, I just need to pull myself together. Every time I get within a five-foot radius you, I'm either crying or coming."

"I prefer the coming." A flash of white crossed his somber face and he closed the small gap between them. "And don't forget the laughing. Damn, I love your smile."

"How long—"

"Shh," he whispered into the curve of her neck, licking and nipping with his teeth. A smooth sensual groan crooned from her throat. "We're not gonna talk. We're not gonna discuss how long or tomorrow." John lifted his elbow, bumping off the light switch.

"Hey, wait, I like seeing you." Her complaint went unheard as he stripped off her shirt, devouring her shoulder.

"I want you to remember right now. Forever." John shimmied her jeans to the ground and lifted her on the counter. He brought her hands to his face, brushing a kiss to the palm of her hand. "It's just you and me, soaring a mile above any land mass. Nothing else matters, Shay. Nothing. I've never felt so connected to anyone as I feel with you."

Minutes passed by in dignified slowness, engulfing her senses in John's texture and spicy scent. Blindly, she worked at his clothing. Laying her hands on his bare chest, she rejoiced in the warmth. The chill of her fingers brought a layer of goose bumps to his skin. John's lower abdomen strained taut as she unbuttoned his jeans, loosening the denim over his hips.

They traced each other's bodies in long, sweeping strokes, filled with intuitive fixation. Each flexing chord and rope in his muscles brought a new thrill to her fingers. A rapacious growl hummed in her throat as her hands roamed lower over his chiseled stomach.

"I love the sounds you make." The moist heat of his heavy breath settled on her skin like a ray of sunshine. The palm of his hands skimmed across her chest, cupping her breasts. He rolled her nipples gently between his finger and thumb. John scooted her to the edge, gently nudging into her wet folds.

She groaned, spreading her legs wider, propping a foot on the wall beside them.

He impaled her, driving deeper.

Shayla wriggled and panted, contracting around him.

He withheld any movement, driving her to near madness before thrusting again. "Oh, yes."

So fully indulged in her euphoric high, she didn't even feel embarrassed of the gratitude oozing in her voice.

A dark, insatiable chuckle rumbled in her ear and he held still again, starving off her climax.

"I can't get enough of you. Part of me wants to make love to you sweet and slow and the other part—" His mouth found hers, firm and slippery. Placing one hand beneath her butt and the other on the mirror behind her back for leverage, he filled her again and again, possessing her mind, body and soul. "—wants to fuck you into the next atmosphere."

A familiar vision flashed in her mind. The same vision she'd had on the flight to Greece. Surrounded by the darkness, she'd never seen him more clearly. A bolt of heat shot through her. Surrendering to his inexorable rhythm, she let her momentum surge and she buried her cries into his mouth. He didn't have to ask to say it. His name rolled off her lips in a long drawn out climax. "John."

****

Saying goodbye to John in Las Vegas was the most difficult thing she had ever done in her life.

Tracy and JC took turns giving her hugs goodbye. Shayla couldn't manage one solitary word, fearing she would have a break down.

JC embraced her, assuring quietly, "Don't worry. Everything happens for a reason."

John held to her tightly with his chin resting on the top of her head, swaying gently while the girls gathered their belongings.

Watching him walk off the plane, not knowing when she would hear from him again, sent a sickening feeling freefalling to the bottom of her gut. They made no plans, no arrangements, no agreements. Crossing her arms over her chest, she couldn't ignore the ache settling behind her heart.

Never in her life had her heart felt completely vacant as the moment she watched him step off the plane. She closed her eyes to visualize him and a flood of sorrow overwhelmed her. Shayla retreated down the aisle, and her quiet sobs filled the empty cabin. Shaking from head to toe, she wept in agony, unable to stop the upsurge of tears.

Suddenly, rough, heavy hands touched her shoulders and John folded her into his arms. He cradled her face. "Shh. Don't cry, baby."

Shayla's chin crumpled and her stomach tangled in confusion. "What are you doing?"

"Giving you something to think about," he said in a guttural voice. In one, smooth, deliberate move, he covered her mouth with his. Huge tears rolled down the side of her nose, catching in his palms. The taste of salt mixed with the minty flavor of his kisses. His tongue sank into her mouth, the sweet heat calming her shredded nerves. Her balance disintegrated and she clung to the hard planes of his body.

Shayla showered him with intoxicating kisses,

showing him the words he didn't want to hear.

John eased away from the warmth of her lips, his eyes fixed upon hers, demanding her full attention. "I want you to know, you're not a reason or a season, Shay. *You* are the woman of a lifetime. I know it will take a few days, but I'll be waiting for your call."

****

Over the next two days, Shayla felt off center in her world. She couldn't stop the despondent feeling of mourning consuming her. She was lost without John. Carrie Ann stayed with her the first night she got home. Shayla sipped on a rock glass of whiskey, pouring her heart out. Her best friend took it all in, but remained speechless.

"Say something. You're freaking me out."

"I'm not sure what to say. I'm still stuck on the fact you…you just kinda went for it. You've been my best friend for ten years and you've *never* gone to bed with a man without dating him for at least a few weeks. I've never seen you make rash decisions." Carrie Ann's bright blue eyes sparkled empathetically. "Typically, you leave the impulse lays to me. Especially the younger ones."

"He's not a lay," she snapped defensively, a scowl tugging between her brows.

"Oh, honey," —Carrie Ann clinked her glass to Shayla's—"I know he's not a lay. It sounds like he's the man of your dreams."

Shayla nodded hotly taking another slow draw from the glass.

"When does Mat get home? I don't envy you, he's not going to take it very well."

"Two days."

Two days felt more like two years. The rising

sun broke over the horizon, and surfers dotted the frigid water, waiting for the perfect wave. Not even the soothing sound of the waves crashing on the beach made her happy. Over the last few days, work left her in a state of exhaustion, yet sleep escaped her. She sat on top her surfboard and closed her eyes, letting her hands drift across the surface of the water. Shayla felt the imprint of John's hands caressing her in the darkness like the water lapping at her thighs.

"Shayla!" A female voice carried along a ripple of water, pulling her from her solitude. A young woman paddled up beside her. Shayla had seen her surfing on several occasions during the summer months. "Congratulations! I was hoping you'd be out here catching some waves today."

A jolt of panic jumped in the center of her chest. "Congratulations?"

"Yeah. Heard Tommy finally got married!"

"What?" Shayla's mouth dropped open, partially relieved the girl wasn't wishing her cheers to marital bliss.

"My mom's a hot mess! She's always had the hots for him. Hey, is she pregnant or what?"

"What? No! Where did you hear that?" Shayla didn't bother waiting for her response. She laid flat and started to paddle for the next wave.

The coarse sand beneath her feet couldn't come fast enough. This was not good. Shayla had spent the last two days arranging interviews and releases, but nothing was scheduled for another week. Everyone assumed her Uncle would be publicizing a new film production or a humanitarian effort. No one would ever guess Tommy Clemmins would be announcing an engagement, let alone a wedding. Tommy wanted complete control when he broke the story about his wedding.

With each pump of her arm, she went over every conversation, hoping she hadn't inadvertently let something slip. She hit the beach running, not even bothering to rinse off the saltwater.

As she rounded the corner for home, her frantic heartbeat dropped to her toes when she caught a glimpse of a black sedan parked out front of her house. "Shit! Not now. I can only deal with one catastrophe at a time."

As she neared her driveway, a driver stepped out and stood outside the door.

Her stomach eddied. She'd gone over her speech with Mat a thousand times, but it didn't make it any easier.

"Mrs. Huntston would like a word with you." The stone-faced driver extended his hand to retrieve her board and opened the car door.

"Mrs. Huntston?" Shayla felt the blood draining from her face as she tilted her head, peering into the car. She opened her mouth to ask if Mat was okay, but was quickly swathed in a negative aura. "Umm, I don't really want to ruin your interior with my wetsuit. Would you like to come in?"

"How considerate of you." Antagonism surged from her pursed lips in whitecaps and her hard glare never faltered from the back of the driver's headrest. "But this won't take long."

Shayla couldn't shake the feeling she'd just been called into the Dean's office. She climbed into the car, awkwardly sitting at the edge of her seat. A hint of the ocean mixed with new car smell as she tucked a sandy, sodden strand of hair behind her ear.

Mat's mother gripped a manila envelope. She opened it and handed a stack of photos to Shayla. "It appears you've been very busy the last week."

A hostile chill hung between them. Shayla's stomach felt like it dropped off a thirty-foot wave as it crashed beneath her. She thumbed through six photos of her with John in Greece. One picture was taken the first day in Greece while they walked innocently through the village. However, several shots were taken at the dock showing them nose-to-nose in an embrace, and two were from the airport of them kissing.

"You had me followed?" she questioned blandly.

"I know a bad egg when I smell one."

"You had no right to follow me. This is between Mat and I." Guilt and contempt mixed with anger at the invasion of her privacy.

"You are nothing but a dirty little tramp," Mrs. Huntston glowered indignantly. "Worthless, like the rest of your family."

Shayla's eyes narrowed. It'd taken years of therapy, but she'd learned to stop taking shit from bullies a long time ago. She forced a casual shrug. "I don't think we should judge each other's families. What do you want?"

"I want you out of my son's life. He has a great political career ahead of him and you are not going to sabotage it," she fumed, jabbing her fingernail into the seat beside her.

"I planned on telling Mat as soon I returned from Greece."

"You won't get the chance. I'm handling it from here on out. I'll be tactful. Do you understand? I don't need your whoring around to get out to the media. You'll make him look like a fool."

Shayla had heard enough. Keeping her cool,

she opened the door and stepped out of the car. The driver shut the door. Her hands trembled violently. Taking control of her surfboard, she fumbled with the photos, dropping one on the ground. The car pulled away from the driveway as she bent to pick up the picture. Peering down at the photo of her and John at the dock, she realized it was taken the day of the wedding.

An idea weaved an unsettling path through her consciousness. "Son-of-a-bitch. The fucking Frenchman! I knew it!"

She laid her board on the ground and trotted barefoot after the car, knocking on the window. The dark tint lowered partially. "Did you really think he wouldn't find out? I suggest you start worrying about the life left in your campaign, Mrs. Huntston. When Tommy finds out you're the one who leaked his wedding, he'll show you no mercy."

"I don't know what you're referring to."

"Oh, I think you know *exactly* what I'm talking about! This picture," —Shayla held up the photo and tossed all of them through the window onto the bitch's lap— "was taken the night of Tommy's wedding. Your investigator sold photos of his wedding just to line his own pocket, to sweeten the deal."

Mrs. Huntston looked as if the full transcript of her concession speech just played through her mind.

Shayla straightened her posture, relishing in the uncomfortable silence. For the first time since Shayla had met her, Mrs. Huntston appeared frazzled.

"I'm guessing you're starting to sweat through that silk blouse right about now."

"I didn't hire an investigator to leak your uncle's wedding. That's ludicrous."

"Actually, I wouldn't refer to it as ludicrous,

more like the demise of your campaign. You may not have hired him to leak Tommy's wedding, but you sure as hell hired him nonetheless. And your dirty little political animal just outed one of Hollywood's most influential players." Shayla enjoyed watching her squirm. Judging by the ashen shade of grey Mrs. Huntston was turning, she was oblivious to the PI's ulterior motives. "I'm assuming you'll make certain Mat will be home tomorrow and that he won't see these photos."

Mrs. Huntston shifted in her seat. She returned the photos to the envelope and curled her fingers into a tight ball on her lap.

"Consider it done," she said insipidly, closing the window and ordering the driver to pull away from the curb.

Shayla worked with her uncle's publicist through the night putting out fires. Tommy and Tess would be arriving earlier than planned. Tommy had an unimaginable wealth of resources, and would dig deep to find the perpetrator...and bury them. How her uncle handled Mrs. Huntston would be his decision, but there was no doubt the woman had just dug her own political grave.

Mat arrived like clockwork the following morning, a dozen white roses in hand. Cupping her elbow, he greeted her with a brief kiss hello. Leaning into his kiss brought the familiar scent of dry-cleaning and body wash. But the feel of his soft lips sparked a new aversion, sending a shudder over her shoulders.

Locking eyes, they both frowned in surprise. "Are you cold?" he asked, moving into the kitchen and opening cabinet to retrieve a clear vase.

She shook her head, somewhat shocked by her

own reaction. Mat wasn't a great kisser, but she'd always found comfort in his kisses. She'd certainly never found them repulsive, until now. Shayla frowned, saddened by the cold, queasy ache building in her throat.

"So what the heck did you do in Greece? Did Tommy really marry that woman?"

She nodded, her heart thudding. "Sorry, I couldn't tell you. We need to talk."

He snipped the bottom of the stems. "Yes, we do," he agreed quietly, filling the clear vase one rose at a time.

By the sensitive tone in his voice, Shayla wondered if his mother had shown him the pictures. "Something happened over the weekend."

Mat snipped the last stem and plunked it into the water. He paused, a tightly puckered brow creased across his forehead when he faced her. "Are you asking me or telling me that something happened over the weekend?"

"I met someone in Greece," she professed warily, carefully watching his reaction through wet lashes. "I'm sorry. I didn't mean to, it just…happened."

His shoulders dropped and he let out a huge sigh. He handed her the damp paper towel he held and she blew her nose. Mat had never seen her cry, seeming shocked by her tears. "Don't cry. It's okay."

"I know, but I hate telling you and I don't want to hurt your feelings. It—"

"Let's sit down. I need to tell you a few things too." Mat looked into her woeful face and let out another sigh of what sounded like relief. Placing his hand on her shoulder, he ushered her to the couch. "You go first and calm down. I'm not mad, Shayla. Just tell me what happened."

She sat beside him, perched on the edge of the couch.

He took one of her hands in his. "I think we might need a shot of Jack Daniels."

She sniffled and shook her head. "I spent the weekend with Tess's son, John. It just happened. I feel horrible and guilty, but we're just not meant to be. I can't marry you. We don't want the same things in life—"

"You're right. We're not meant to be."

His reserved reaction sent a ripple of guilt down her spine. She cringed a bit. She felt him trembling, and a clammy layer of moisture covered his hands.

"I met someone this weekend too, in Washington."

A ticklish skitter traipsed through her abdomen, partly shocked and somewhat relieved. "You did? Have you seen her before or was this the first time?"

Mat's lips pursed and he blew out a long drawn out puff of air. "I know I can trust you, Shayla. God, you're about the only person I can really trust. I know this is going to hurt you and I want you to know that that was never my intension." Mat seemed to be in agony watching her cry. "I think I'm gay."

"What?" Her head automatically shirked back in disbelief. Shayla's lashes fluttered repeatedly and she hopped up from the couch. "Gay? What? How long have you been gay? Are you sure?"

"Before you get upset, let me explain." He tugged on her fingers, encouraging her to sit. "This weekend was the first time. I experimented once in college, but it never got off the ground. I can't tell you how horrible I've felt the last two days, knowing

I had to come clean to you. But for the first time in my life, Shayla, I feel…right inside."

Her mouth opened then closed. "I think we are definitely going to need the Jack."

As she processed the information, reflecting on bits and pieces of their relationship, things began to make sense now. He followed her to the kitchen, retrieving two rock glasses and loading them with ice.

Shayla poured them each a stiff drink and smiled thoughtfully. "To our non-engagement."

"To our non-engagement."

The sweet slow burn coated her throat. She couldn't help but notice how relaxed Mat seemed, like a boulder had been lifted off his shoulders. How horrible it would be to live in denial, to feel the weight of fearing acceptance. As the thought furrowed through her mind, she saw her father's face. She understood what it was like to hide certain aspects of your life so people couldn't see deep inside your story.

"God, I have so many questions." Smiling sheepishly, she asked earnestly, "Was it wonderful? I mean, if you've had urges and thoughts before, was it what you expected it to be?"

"Are you seriously asking? I don't know if we should talk about it," he said candidly. "The last thing I want to do is hurt your feelings."

"Mat, you were my friend first. I'm really asking."

He paused. "Imagine if *you'd* been having sex with a woman all these years and then you tried out a man." Mat nodded, clinking her glass again. Appreciation shimmered in his bright blue eyes. "Not that there was anything wrong with you or our sex. You were always—"

Shayla held up a hand. "It's obvious to me now we had a relationship of convenience. I was able to hide from the past and you were able to hide from the present," she acknowledged in a low voice, a bit of sadness mixing with understanding.

"I'm sorry I haven't been the boyfriend you needed me to be. I hope you don't feel like our relationship was a waste of two years of your life."

"I don't feel that way at all. Some things happen at a particular time for a certain reason. The weekend seemed to be perfect timing for both of us. Honestly, I just want you to be happy."

"Do you really like him? Tess's son?"

"John. Yes, he's amazing." Her eyes held wide and she nodded slowly. "Your mother knows."

"Believe me, she has no idea I'm gay." The word *gay* rolled off his tongue in triumph, as if it was the biggest achievement of his life to say the word out loud. He shot a swig of whiskey, washing down the ghastly notion. "And I have no idea how I'm going to break the truth to her. Or when."

"Your mother knows about me, about my affair with John. There's more I need to tell."

They continued their open dialogue, each sharing vulnerabilities they'd never exposed to each other before. The wall that had been built up over the last few years by false pretenses came crumbling down, spurring a new bond of friendship. Shayla came to the understanding that their relationship had always been more about suitability than love. She'd never expected her connection with Mat to be passionate and he never pushed to know about her past.

He apologized repeatedly for his mother's actions regarding the private investigator. She appreciated his kind words, but knew all too well he couldn't control his mother's actions. However, one thing was certain: it wouldn't be Mat's sexuality that would cripple his mother's campaign. It would be her own malicious cruel intentions.

After a few hours of lengthy conversation and a cup of hot coffee, she walked Mat to the door. A simple act of saying goodbye they'd done hundreds of times changed as he held her close. Swathed in his full embrace she knew, for the first time in his life, Mat was comfortable in his own skin.

****

Shayla tried calling and texting John over the next few days, but was sent straight to voice mail with no return text. She wondered if he was out walking the streets of Las Vegas barefoot or simply ignoring her. By the fourth day, she was fully annoyed and worried sick. Tommy and Tess had arrived the day before, and fortunately, Shayla was so busy dealing with entertainment producers and stalking paparazzi, that she didn't have much time to dwell on John.

"Don't worry, there's probably just no reception where he's at," Tracy said when she called asking for copies of pictures taken at the wedding. "When you didn't call him for two days, he texted me saying he was taking off for Utah."

"He knew I wasn't going to be able to see Mat for at least a day or two." She couldn't contain the urgency or irritation in her tone. Shayla added defensively, "I ended things with Mat."

"There's a little more to it than that. Yesterday was our dad's birthday." Tracy cleared the sentiment from her throat. "John and my dad used to do an annual ride this time of year in Moab. My guess is, he just couldn't deal with everything going on all at once, so he took off. We all miss our dad. And don't take this the wrong way, we love Tom and we are ridiculously happy for our mom, but the wedding was little bitter sweet. It's the start of something new and wonderful, yet it's also closing another door. The wedding just wreaked a little havoc on our emotions, that's all. None of us even realized it until we got home to the *house*. Then JC and I left the next day. We had to fly back to school in Colorado for exams."

"I'm sorry," Shayla said uneasily. "I was so happy for them I didn't look at it from your prospective. Not to mention I couldn't see three feet beyond your brother."

"John's used to getting what he goes after. He's usually chasing goals not a woman, but regardless, he just sets his mind to something and works hard until he gets it." Amusement laced her tone. "He wants you! Poor guy had a melt down after we got off the plane."

"If you talk to him, would you mind asking him to please call me?"

"I doubt I'll hear from him before you. We're heading straight from school to the cabin. But if I do, I'll mention we talked. My mom would never forgive him if he didn't make it to the cabin for Christmas, so don't worry. He'll show up."

"Thanks. See you in a few days," she murmured, dizzy with anticipation and nerves.

CHAPTER TWELVE

If Shayla could've summed up the definition of the word *forever*, it would've been her flight from LA to Colorado. She received one text from John two days before.

Sorry I made you worry. I'll see you at the cabin. I miss you.

She was so irritated by the time she got his text, all she could say back was *I'll see you at the cabin.* It took a whole two minutes longer before she sent another text. *I miss you, too.*

By this point, her brain sizzled, fried from emotional overload and sheer exhaustion. What few hours of sleep she managed to grab over the last week were full of tossing and turning. She didn't know if John would already be at the cabin or if she'd have to wait to see him.

Shayla missed him immensely, beyond any words of description, yet she tried to contain her excitement. The minute possibility she wasn't even his girlfriend nearly brought her crumbling to her knees. As the flight neared its destination, she paced through the cabin. The attendant finally encouraged her to take her seat for landing.

Dragging herself through a sea of empty faces, she followed the stream of passengers to the luggage claim. Bags dropped into the moving luggage carousel. Shayla hitched her purse strap higher onto her shoulder and squeezed between anxious holiday travelers. She reached for her grey suitcase, yanking it by the handle.

Someone tried to grab her suitcase. She spun around, staring into a familiar pair of broad shoulders. The warmth of John's strong fingers slid over hers, lifting the suitcase with ease and standing it upright. His lips brushed her earlobe, "How many do you have?"

Her pulse rampaged. "Just one."

Passengers bumped and wedged themselves behind her.

She wobbled, molding herself to his front, staring up at him with dizzy surprise. She grumbled breathlessly. "I didn't know if you would come."

John laid his free hand on the small of her back, guiding her away from the carousel. "Of course I was going to come."

They made it ten steps, before she stopped abruptly. She could feel the scarlet coloring creeping up her neck, catching the lobes of her ears on fire. She wiggled free of his hand on her back and faced him head on. Shayla's lip twitched and her chest heaved up and down. "How am I supposed to know that, John? You didn't even call me!"

He reached for her, but she shirked away from his touch. His eyes tapered, accessing her frustration.

Days of worry boiled over, and a flurry of emotions overcame her. "I got one text! One!"

"I'm sorry. I was outta—"

"What? Out of cell range?" Her voice climbed higher. She cut him a sharp look, daring him to argue. "I talked to Tracy. You still should've called!"

His eyes shifted to the crowd taking notice of her outburst. "That's not exactly what I was going to say."

She threw her hands to her hips. "Do you have a better excuse for ignoring me? Torturing me. Driving me crazy?"

"Yes, yes I do."

A small rueful grin floated at the edge of his bold mouth, sending her into an outburst.

"You think this is funny?" she gasped, repeating the words he said in Greece. Her blood boiled over clouding her thoughts. "I have the best weekend of my life and then I don't hear from you! I didn't know if you would be here! I don't even know if we're together! Why the hell—"

"God you're adorable when you're mad." He released the handle of the suitcase and stroked a loose strand of hair behind her ear, tracing it with the tip of his finger.

Every hair on her body rose at the sweetness in his voice. John cast a slow, burning gaze over her face that dismantled her brain, rendering her speechless. The erotic scent of him drew her closer.

"I couldn't call you because I was busy going outta my mind." Both his hands cradled her jaw, caressing her cheeks with the pad of his thumbs. "Because there was no way in hell I was going to tell you how much I love you over a call or text."

Her unrest diminished as he said the words she longed to hear. Every last morsel of space between them evaporated. "You do?"

John nodded, nuzzling into her temple, inhaling the scent of her neck. His lips wandered over her cheeks and neck, working her into a rush of desire. "I love you, Shay."

"I love you too."

Her arms circled around his neck, pulling his lips to hers. She felt the invisible threads biding them as one, each possessing kiss, claiming them as each others.

Cheers and applause broke out around them. She pulled away from him, but only to smile staring into his handsome face. Her eyes dashed from side to side, watching on-goers from ages ten to sixty pulled out their cell phones to take pictures of their affectionate embrace.

Boasting crimson cheeks, they wrapped their arms around each others waists and continued toward the elevators. She stopped and tugged on his fingers so he would face her. Shayla drank in the gorgeous sight of him. Dark, bruising shadows dusted beneath his eyes, but the breathtaking gleam of emerald made her tingle from head to toe.

A quick breath hissed from her lungs as she brought her palm to his cheek. Her fingers played across his stubble. Yearning to feel the rasp on her skin, she let her eyes drift and lashes lower with absolute slowness. "You haven't shaved. I love it."

"I love you, Shay. I'm sorry I didn't call. I almost flew to California. Hell, I probably could've ridden my bike there." His avid eyes tracked the movement of her tongue as she wet her lower lip and drew it between her teeth. "I didn't want to be a charity case, or have you choose me because I made you feel guilty. I just...I needed to know you fell as hard for me as I did you."

Shayla's hands slid inside his open jacket around his waist. She slumped against his solid frame, emotionally drained and completely spent. "Don't ever do that to me again."

"Oh, believe me, we are going to kiss like this every time we're in an airport. The applause was great. It's gonna be our *thing*." His arm curled behind the small of her back. Her arms locked between them and he bent over, ravishing her neck. "Next time I'm gonna bend you over—"he growled into the scoop of her neck " —and dip you."

Her fists clenched the corners of his open collar and tugged as she kissed his chin. "You know damn well what I mean. Don't ever *not* call me. If you go off by yourself—"

"I won't be by myself, Shay. I don't ever want to be without you again. Not for one night."

Without an ounce of hesitation, she agreed. "I don't want to be without you either."

"So that means we've got some figuring to do over Christmas."

****

Shayla had never been a big fan of the holiday season, often comparing it to a root canal: a painful numbing experience that thankfully only lasted a short amount of time, yet cost a small fortune to endure. She had never *enjoyed* Christmas. She suffered through each one with her deranged parents, creating some of her worst childhood memories.

Making their way up the drive, Shayla let out a sound of awe as she caught a glimpse of the cabin tucked into the tree line. Situated just over a small crest from a ski run, the log structure looked more like an intimate resort than a cabin. "Wow."

"Tommy said you've never been here." He gave her a sideways glance and wriggled his brow. "Everyone is on the slopes, so we have the place to ourselves for a few more hours."

Shayla pretended to open her car door before it

had come to a stop, drawing a deep sexy chuckle from John. They unloaded her things, bypassing the luxurious living area and dining room.

A gorgeous thirty-foot tall rock fireplace passed by in a blur.

He made a pit stop in the kitchen, grabbing a couple of waters from the fridge. John abruptly snatched her around the hips and Shayla let out a tiny squeak as her legs automatically wrapped around his hips.

"Thirsty?" she teased sardonically.

"These are for you, baby." John started down the hall with two waters in one hand and her suitcase in the other.

She clung to him like a koala bear. Her hand slipped inside the neck of his shirt indulging in the feel of his muscular back. "You're gonna need them cause I'm taking you to bed and making love to you till we're both delirious. Fuck, I've never missed anyone so desperately in all my life!"

She unabashedly sunk lower, wriggling to feel his arousal, kissing and nibbling the smooth texture at his neck and collar. She pulled in a deep breath, tasting his flavor on her tongue.

He stopped outside a bedroom door and lowered her feet to the floor. "Seriously, Shay. I know we've only spent a long weekend together."

"The most amazing weekend imaginable," she corrected, tugging on his belt loop.

John nodded. "That was just the beginning. I meant what I said. I don't ever want to be without you again. I know it sounds crazy, but I was miserable without you. I felt sick, and I was just empty inside."

Tears welled in her eyes. "I know this sounds

cliché, but I feel…whole with you. Complete."

He kissed her long and hard until they were both deprived of oxygen.

She wiped her mouth with the back of her hand, blushing as she glanced at the door.

"I just assumed or hoped you would be sharing my room. My mom and Tom had a few things already set up in another room for you, but I took the liberty of moving them." He nipped her neckline before opening the door.

"You just took it upon yourself to make decisions for me." A crooked grin played across her face, the sensation of his lips already turning her breathless.

"Would you feel better if I stayed in your room? Mine is at the end of the hall…all by itself." As the last three words rolled sensually off his tongue, John's hand slid down her lower back, curling beneath her cheeks, sending her into near convulsions.

Her eyes rolled back. She didn't have a chance in hell of keeping a straight face. "No. This is perfect."

"That's what I thought."

A king size log bed, dressed in sumptuous white linens, captured her attention. The exterior walls were made of rough, hand-hewn eighteen-inch logs, but a faint sunny yellow washed the smooth textured interior walls. A large arrangement of flowers sitting on a dark table drew her eye. Shayla laughed out loud, sauntering over to inspect the hodgepodge of flowers with half of the buds intentionally pinched off. Her smile broadened as she plucked off another bud, inhaling the sweetness.

"I totally forgot this year."

His heated grin grew as he watched her reaction. "Tommy wouldn't tell me the joke. The only thing I could get out of him was that it was a family tradition."

"The first couple of Christmases Tommy and I had together were hard." Shayla raised the flower to his nose, spinning it between her fingers. "Growing up, my dad sabotaged *every* holiday, and Christmas was the absolute worst. God forbid if anyone wanted to be happy. And if he was expected to buy a present, it was guaranteed to be smashed to pieces by the end of the day."

Her thoughts pulled her back to a faded, but not forgotten memory. John listened attentively as she shared her story. He took the flower, etching it along her chin and tracing the shell of her ear.

"I learned to hide in my room a lot. Anyways, when I moved to California, Tommy didn't really like Christmas either. It was the only day I ever saw him dwell on the fact that he had never married and had a family. He never admitted this, but I always thought Christmas was like a day of mourning for him. I knew he needed his space, so I started having Christmas with my friend Carrie Ann. Tom opted for solitude, making the excuse of researching new films."

"He seems ecstatic this year." John began to unbutton her shirt.

"Must be the love going around." She simmered, holding onto his waist, rolling her thumbs over his tightly packed abs.

"So how do the flowers come into play?"

"Eventually, we joked about it and then it became somewhat of a spoof. I sent him an empty bottle of wine and a container of half eaten cookies wishing him a very Merry Christmas. He volleyed by sending me one new boot, the matching footwear arrived the following day. One year I bought him a great tie, but drizzled ketchup all over it before sticking it in the mail. But my favorite Christmas ever was when he sent me bouquet after bouquet of flowers. The delivery man kept coming back all day until my new house was filled with every species of flower imaginable."

Corralling her against edge of the bed, John let the back of his fingers brush against her abdomen as he unzipped her jeans. The curve of his mouth had nothing to do with humor. He stripped her of her boots, tossing them over his shoulder one at a time before undressing and tackling her on the bed.

They rolled over the fluffy down comforter, entwined in each other's arms. John slipped his palm inside her black lace bra, covering the erect tip of her breast with his mouth. Her fingers ran through his dark locks of hair, gripping tightly as the low ache in her core contracted. He straddled her hips, working over her mouth in long indecent licks of his tongue. A delicious heat surged through her limbs.

John broke the kiss, biting her shoulder gently before easing her onto her stomach. He unclasped her bra and hooked his fingers through her black panties, nearly tearing the lace. "If I remember correctly, you rather liked this."

His voice slipped over her shoulders like crushed velvet.

A simpering camber held to her mouth, twisting to see his face beside hers. "Oh, yes, I did."

Leaning back on his haunches, he wedged a knee between her legs and then another, caressing the back of her leg all the way down to her toes.

"God, I love you."

Feeling the heat of his moist breath on her ass, she trembled and arched.

"You're skin smells so delicious. I've thought about tasting you since I walked off that damn plane."

Each place his body touched hers created a spark of energy. Her hips arched upward in a primal craving, as if they had a mind of their own. Every timid insecurity she'd known dissolved in his presence. He rubbed up the back of her thighs as his mouth wondered over the ticklish spot at the small of her back. Her hips rose higher and she bucked a little, needing more. "John, please," she panted in a raspy voice.

A small knowing grumble came from his throat and he took a tender bite of her ass. His thumbs put pressure on the inside of her thighs, lifting her a few inches higher. "You missed me."

"Yes." Her voice strained taut in unbearable desire.

Her heart slammed erratically in eagerness. A long swipe of his tongue pierced through her soft flesh. She shivered at the sensation of his mouth languidly feeding off her. Her heartbeat rocked through her veins and she balled her fists in the bedding. Waves of pleasure rolled, building and climbing. She reached her hand between her thighs to rub her aching flesh, but he grabbed her, lacing his fingers through hers, pinning it to the bed.

"Wait," came a guttural sound of command. She writhed beneath his masterful mouth, her pulse brutal in its force. He teased her, deliberately avoiding the one spot she so badly needed him to flick.

Her head thrashed back and forth. "Can't."

He marauded deeper, getting closer, bringing

her to a height of fervor she'd never known. Her heart slammed and she clenched in anticipation.

"John!"

He delivered, plunging deep inside, drawing her cleft into the searing heat of his mouth. Shudders wracked her body, pushing her into rapture.

His hot, wet mouth laid down a torturous trail of nibbles and bites along her back. "That is how much I missed you, baby."

She collected her breath and stretched out her cramped fingers that were clenched tightly to the sheets.

He lowered on top of her back, the warmth of his body blanketing her damp skin. He rubbed his hands over each of hers, interlacing his thick fingers between hers, holding his crushing weight on his elbows. Her inner muscles contracted in acceptance as she felt the gentle nudge of his erection gliding over her silken folds.

His breath came in hungry pants beside her cheek.

Shayla twisted, opening her mouth, rooting for his kisses.

"Easy," he whispered, taking in her tongue.

Her rising moan filled their mouths and she shivered, tasting her own essence on his breath.

He gave a low, guttural groan of pleasure, holding her gaze until he entered her.

Shayla gripped tighter to his fingers, slippery from sweat, accepting the thick fullness of him. She clenched around him, marveling at the feel of his erection as he pushed deeper into her wet heat.

His face was right beside hers. She loved the way his eyes turned cloudy in a passion-filled daze. He rocked into her again and again, taking in every nuance of her reaction, learning from each whimper. Her teeth nipped at his skin and her parted lips dragged over the flexing muscles of his arm and shoulder.

Nuzzling into her neck, John released her fingers and gripped her hips, lifting them higher.

Shayla's head lowered, allowing her to scrunch deeper into the folds of the bedding. Her hips shifted backward, greeting his thrusts. She began to peak and sounds of excitement rose from her throat in pleasure.

John tangled one hand into her mane of hair and the other gripped her shoulder, impaling her in a tireless rhythm until they both came in hard shudders. He crumpled on top of her, falling off to one side, pulling her body close to his. Swamped with emotions, she snuggled into his chest.

Swathed in sheets holding the salty essence of sex and skin, both were too exhausted to speak.

Shayla lay in the crook of his arm, lazily fingering the dark curls on his chest.

His hands lingered over her bare hip in idle circles.

She was happier than she had been in her entire life. There was no place else she would ever want to be.

"I know you can't leave your job, but I can do my job from any computer. I'll need to get some of my things before we go to Vegas. We'll work out the rest later. I just want to be wherever you are." Her quiet words were tucked between a few yawns as she began to drift off.

John pulled the blanket higher and pressed his lips to her hair. "Thank you."

CHAPTER THIRTEEN

A large, luminous star on the side of the mountain marked the coming of Christmas. Shayla wondered if Old Saint Nick himself was going to emerge from the fireplace on Christmas morning, covered in soot in search of chocolate chip cookies and milk. She'd seen the jolly man dressed in his red suit and white beard on the ski slopes, on a snow mobile, and shoveling snow along a drive.

Everyone came and went on their own schedules, skiing, sledding, tubing, and shopping. The list of fun was never ending. The Levi's arrived, bringing a whole new dynamic to the festivities, especially with their seven-year-old daughter, Kim. If she wasn't at ski school, she was stuck to JC's side like duct tape, sporting footed reindeer pajamas and an antler hat.

Shayla felt like she had stepped into an old fashioned Christmas postcard. The week that followed was like living in a dream. Neither Shayla nor John came prepared with presents in tow, so they spent a few mornings snowboarding and a few afternoons shopping for the perfect gifts. The small Colorado ski town redefined the term *decked out for the holidays*.

Shayla and John strolled arm-in-arm through the streets the day before Christmas Eve. The sound of sleigh bells mixed with the sweet songs of carolers, as horse-drawn sleighs paraded passengers down the quaint streets.

Snowflakes began to fall and the icy crystals collected on their lashes and lips. "Please tell me we're coming back here next year?"

A sexy smile tugged at his mouth. He pulled his hand from his jacket and wiped a flake from her lip with the ball of his warm thumb. "We're definitely coming back here next year."

"Seriously, is this not just the best?" Shayla stopped in the middle of the sidewalk, holding her arms out wide. Big snowflakes gathered on her shoulders and knitted hat. She motioned to the street ahead, lined with never-ending rows of twinkle lights, and light poles adorned in wreaths. "I mean look! I feel like I'm in a life-size gingerbread village."

He shot her a stealthy grin. "Wait till you see what I have in store for you tomorrow."

John and Shayla spent Christmas Eve morning on the slopes. Both of them were avid snowboarders. However, neither could keep up with JC or the Levi's. Shayla gave up trying after two runs and the double black diamond.

JC promised it would be a piece of cake, but after a few falls, Shayla felt more like a smushed flapjack, and at one point thought she might have to walk down.

Everyone met back at the cabin for an early afternoon dinner. The unmistakable aroma of homemade pies filled the cabin when they walked in after snowboarding. The kitchen counter was buried beneath all of the homemade goodness.

Tess hovered over the oven, removing perfectly toasted apple pies, and Tracy sat on a barstool snacking on moosemunch.

"Can I help?"

"Awe, thanks, sweetie, but I've got it," Tess said.

"Are you sure?"

Tracy patted the seat next to her. "She cooks, we do clean up. It's tradition."

"Oh. Okay." Shayla climbed onto the stool, grabbing a slice of cheese and topping it on a cracker.

"Damn, it smells good in here." Tommy's praise and wide smile brought a blush to Tess's cheeks. His arms encircled her from behind and he placed a kiss of affection on her cheek.

Tracy and Shayla smiled at each other, witnessing the simple intimate act.

"How was boarding?"

"Me?" Shayla pointed to her chest. "It was great."

"Between them and you and John, I feel like I need a boyfriend," Tracy grumbled, taking dishes to the table. She hollered down the stairway to the basement as she headed for the dining room, "Time to eat!"

Everyone gathered at the long rustic table cut from a six-inch slab of wood. Delectable dishes lined the table, nestled between a gorgeous candelabra made of iron.

John pulled out Shayla's chair, tucking it beneath her.

She glanced around the table, and for the first time in her life, Shayla felt like she belonged to a real family. Her heart brimmed full and her chest felt heavy. Sentiments of love mixed with a deep seeded feeling of peace. Every book she read as a little girl filled with Christmas magic could not have prepared her for the real, true feeling welling in her heart.

She sniffled, capturing John's attention. His eyes slipped over her in his peripheral view and he casually placed his hand on her leg, handing her his napkin. She stared at her plate, not wanting to draw attention to herself, blotting her nose with the napkin. When she thought she had a handle on it, Shayla looked up to see Tommy watching her.

He looked a bit weepy too, and she broke. Silent tears flowed down her cheeks.

She sniffed again, giving a small chuckle of embarrassment, shaking her finger at Tommy as a playful warning not to make her cry.

JC wrenched her head forward, peering down the table. "Are you crying?"

Shayla shook her head in innocent denial and then nodded, laughing at her own silliness. "Sorry."

Before she had time to excuse herself, JC leaned over her, wrapping her in the sweetest hug. "It's okay, don't cry."

Shayla's shoulders shook from laughing and crying. "I'm okay. I'm happy. It's just that this has been such a wonderful holiday."

John smiled at her over JC's arm.

JC smooched her cheek, whispering in her ear, "I knew this was going to happen."

Shayla snickered a little between sniffles, watching JC tug her phone from her back pocket. She flipped though pictures, pulling up the picture of photo of John and Shayla asleep on the flight to Greece. The picture had a heart and the word *Christmas* written across it, drawn by the tip of her finger with a phone app. "See? I knew it!"

A grateful smile lingered with doubt. "Manifesting again?"

"Umm hmm."

After dinner, the girls pitched in to clear the table and do dishes.

John stole Shayla away in the midst, assuring her they'd make breakfast for everyone the next morning. He held out her snowboarding suit. "Don't ask, just put it on."

Shayla did as he asked and slipped into her gear without uttering a single word.

Stepping out into the frigid night air, they strapped into their snowboards. Falling snow covered the well-beaten path between the towering pines. They cut their way through the powder, taking the trail toward the slopes. Frigid night air pinched her cheeks and the scraping sound of their boards filled the still night.

When they made it out the chute and past the tree-line, John stopped, pulling a blanket from his backpack. Careful not to disturb the dense branches loaded with heavy snow, he tucked the thick blanket beneath the pine, sheltering them from the falling snow.

"What are we doing?"

"We're waiting."

John stretched out long on his side on top of the blanket. Shayla dug the edge of her board into the powder and dropped to her bottom, leaning against his abs for support. He took off one glove and retrieved a silver flask of whiskey from his inside pocket.

"Have a told you how much I love you?" she said, taking a swig, letting the burn of the whiskey warm her from the inside. She cocked her head, listening. Voices carried through the treetops and light falling snow. "Is that...singing?"

He snuggled closer. "Umm hmm."

Within minutes, torch-bearing skiers began making their way down the mountain. Hoots and hollers rang out between lyrics of jingle bells and ho-ho-ho's as the parade of lights made it's way down the mountainside. Colorful illuminations took the traditional form of a Christmas tree as the skiers and snowboarder crossed side to side across, cruising down the slope.

A loud crack thundered in the darkness and fireworks shot through the night sky. Barely visible through the winter wonderland, an exploding star burst over the top of the Christmas tree with each boom. "Merry Christmas Eve, Shay."

She slouched, kissing him through three rounds of star burst. "Merry Christmas Eve. Thank you."

"You're welcome."

****

Cool morning air whispered across the heated flush of her body. Shayla and John lay tangled in bed while the sun pushed through the shuttered window. Sex mingled with the morning scent of their warm bodies. "Merry Christmas, baby," John purred into the folds of her hair.

"Merry Christmas." Shayla rolled over, settling into the now familiar moldings of his torso, feeling safe, happy and loved. Her fingers keyed rhythmically across his collarbone. "What's your favorite Christmas memory?"

"This is my favorite, right now." He stroked down her back, the tip of his finger barely connecting with her skin, making her giggle and squirm.

Shayla knew John's life was filled with fond

family memories, but she noticed he kept quiet while his sisters told story after story, reminiscing Christmases past. She crawled on top of him, stretching out flat on the length of his body. He closed his eyes as he tucked his hands behind his head. She shimmied up his chest so she could kiss his chin.

"John, I want to hear you talk about your life, your family, and all of the wonderful memories you have. I grew up thinking those bonds weren't possible. I love you, and I love your sisters and your mom, too. Hearing those stories and being around your family, makes me feel good inside. Not jealous. Okay, maybe a tiny bit envious, but it makes me have faith in that kind of love, knowing it's possible."

"Honestly, I think I've died and gone to heaven right now, Shay. At this moment, with you lying all naked and warm across my body, staring up at me with your big beautiful eyes." He fingered through her tussles of hair. "The Christmas sun is shining through the shutters, casting pieces of light over your bare shoulders. Baby, I've never had a better moment in my life than the one I'm having right now."

Her chest grew tight and her nose tickled
The heat between them turned blistering.

"My family isn't perfect, Shay, but you're right, I have been holding back. I didn't want to hurt your feelings." He rolled, pinning her beneath him, his firm thighs anchoring her to the mattress. "And *we* have a lifetime of wonderful memories ahead of us."

A smile lit up Shayla's face. "John, this is my first best-Christmas memory."

"I've got a better one for you." John kissed her, hungrily and open-mouthed. Caught in a ray of morning sun, they stared keenly into each other's faces, indulging in the joy of pure pleasure, making love and savoring, in that precise moment, the making of a memory that would last a lifetime.

****

Christmas day was spent gathered around the beautiful tree and massive rock fireplace. Everyone relished in a day of relaxation, appreciating the down time with family and good friends.

John and Shayla lounged in their pajamas all day shooting pool, playing cards, eating, sleeping and making love. Christmas took on a whole new meaning for Shayla. It was no longer be a day she dreaded that stirred up ugly memories from her past, it was a day filled with love and family. A day that she would look forward to every year.

Tommy and Tess snuck out early the morning after Christmas for their official honeymoon in Bora Bora and the Levi's left that afternoon for Germany to finish filming a movie.

The week that followed was undoubtedly the best time of her life. According to his sisters, John's acquired most of his looks, habits and mannerism from their father, Richard, including the life motto *work hard, play hard*. And he showed it. He talked passionately about his work and gave thorough inspections to each and every structure they entered. One evening as they enjoyed dinner at a slope-side resort, John stared up at the thirty-foot ceiling, pointing out enormous rafters and huge saddles made from black iron, screwed together with twelve-inch lag bolts.

Shayla took interest, listening intently, but the terminology sent her thoughts straight to the gutter. The man had the uncanny ability to make her break out in a misty layer of heat that spread crimson over her cheeks with the mere curl of his smile.

"Stop. You're seriously turning me on," she snickered and he smothered a laugh into the curve of her neck.

As vacation came to an end, they spent their last day on the slopes. A large snowstorm kept them inside for two days after Christmas, and they wanted to make the most of their last day boarding. They started the day with Tracy and JC, catching the hopper Gondola and zig-zagging their way to the top of peak seven. After hitting a black diamond called The Abominable Snowman, the foursome turned into a twosome, losing the girls — or at least JC — to some hot snowboarders.

John and Shayla packed the glorious day with run after run, crisscrossing their way to peak nine, where they stopped and ate lunch. Making their way back across three mountain peaks, they found the girls and two very handsome men from ski patrol waiting at the base of the super chair.

After JC exchanged numbers with one of the young men, they all caught the lift for one last run. JC filled the ride with chatter about the boys she'd met, seeming hopeful to have dinner with the one she'd just given her number to.

John remained somewhat quiet regarding his sister's harmless flirting, uttering a few scoffs.

Shayla was thrilled to see a blue sign reading Spruce Alley, thankful their last ride wasn't another black diamond. Most of the skiers and boarders had already packed it in, leaving only a few catching the last runs of the day. Massive green spruce trees bordered the narrow pass. The echoes of their voices and the carving of their boards carried through the trees. Shayla relaxed back into her heels, squeezing every ounce of enjoyment out of their last run.

Halfway down the mountain, they paused at the tree line to take in the gorgeous view of the city below.

John pointed to a double chair lift at the intersection of the main run.

"Hey, we'll meet you at the bottom. Shayla and I are gonna take one more run," John called out to his sisters. The tone in his voice gave a warning that wasn't an invitation.

Shayla started to tire and sighed, glancing toward the chair.

A soft smile tugged at the corner of his mouth. "It's Lover's Lane."

"In that case..." Shayla smiled and pushed off, meeting him at the chair.

They were the last riders of the day. The chair bumped the back of her legs and she sat back, snuggling in beside him. The chair gradually lifted them high above the snow-covered ground, carrying them through a cut channel of tall trees. The sun set behind the larger peaks to the west, casting a grey shadow over the snow.

She peeled off a glove and unsnapped her helmet. Sticking to her chair routine, she blew her nose and applied a minty balm to her dry lips, kissing him softly to share the creamy relief. "What a great day."

"What a great *week*." John closed his eyes and inhaled deeply, then blew out his breath in a cloudy whisper of air.

The tension of the cable hummed and creaked, transporting them higher toward the peak. Bows of the spruce trees whispered and groaned as a gust eddied between them, swirling the snow from the branches.

Shayla let her head fall back, leaning against his

shoulder, taking in the still sounds of Mother Nature.

"Shay?" He reached for her bare hand, clasping it in his.

"Hmm?" Her lashes remained shut and she smiled, happy in her moment of solitude, thankful he'd suggested the ride.

"Do you ever just know when something is right?" he asked softly.

Shayla opened her eyes, peering up into his handsome face. Her hand crept up, brushing the snow crystals from the short hairs of his beard above his lip. "You mean that tranquil feeling of calm inside?"

"Umm hmm."

"Feelings of an emotion you just can't put your finger on, or give a word to?" She let out a tiny chuckle. "That feeling that might make you cry for no apparent reason."

His eyes held a small smile, but his mouth held firm. "Yes."

"There's a possibility I might have acquired this capability recently," she teased, gazing up at him, wanting him to kiss her.

He let go of her hand and reached into the inside pocket of his jacket. Pinched between his fingers, he held a ring. John stared at the white gold band, topped with a gorgeous diamond.

Shayla's heart stopped as she stared at the beautiful stone glittering in the setting sun. A warm feeling of adoration and protection fell over her like the hushed silence blanketing the forest that surrounded them.

John shifted his intense focus back to her. Shayla stared back, mesmerized by the love swirling in his green eyes.

"This is the ring my father gave to my mother over twenty-five years ago." Pools welled in his eyes.

She watched his chest rise and fall beneath to open zipper of his ski jacket. Hot tears streamed down her frigid cheeks.

John cleared his throat. "This ring represents a lifetime of a great love, a magical love that I only hoped to know and understand one day. Today is that day, Shay. I don't need time to decipher if you're the one. You *are* the one." He smiled as tears gathered at the corner of his lashes. "My dad used to tell me the story of the very first time he saw my mom. God, he loved her. I'd heard it so many times that I always wondered if it was just a silly story, until I walked onto that airplane."

"I was so mad at you for beating up Tommy." Shayla's chest jumped as she giggled. She saw a flash of his white smile though her tears.

"Shay, you are the woman of a lifetime. My lifetime."

She nodded blindly. "Our lifetime."

"Marry me, Shayla?" He stroked the tears from her face. "Come home with me, we'll get a place, get married, start a life together, travel, get a dog" — he pressed his forehead to hers — "make babies. I want to do it all with you." John cradled her face with the ring still in his fingers. Throwing his head back, he yelled through the canyon, "Shayla Clemmins, will you marry me?"

"Just so you have a great ending for our story when you tell it to our kids," — she raised her chin to the sky — "yes! I will marry you, John Mathews!"

John slipped the timeless engagement ring on her finger and took her mouth in a toe curling kiss. They remained lip-locked until it was time to get off the lift.

As they slipped off the chair, the ski attendant standing at the warming hut waved with a big smile. "Congratulations! Have a great run!"

"Thank you!" John and Shayla waved back, beaming with pride as they dropped off to one side of the slope to strap their boots into their boards.

He brought her face to his, smiling and kissing and crying at the same time. "Let's get out of here."

A loud, thunderous crack followed by a *whumpf* startled them.

Time turned in slow motion as John's lashes closed and opened. His green eyes, swathed in terror, locked to the loud sound of snapping trees coming from behind.

"Strap in, Shay. Strap in, baby." His desperate commands muffled as her pulse turned wild, rioting through her veins. Each of them bent, fingers working desperately to get her boot locked. "Fuck, strap in!"

Shayla's head twisted and she caught sight of the fear in his eyes. Her perception of time slowed, stretching out the scene hurtling toward them. "I can't! Just go! I'm trying—"

The snow moved, collapsing beneath them, and suddenly John was gone.

Shayla was swept away in a wall of white and darkness with no time to react. The wave of white bore down, leaving them at the mercy of the avalanche. Thrown to her belly from the force of the snow, her instinct to swim kicked in. Her arms paddled, trying to find the surface, but her movements flailed aimlessly in the heavy slabs and dense powder.

Her board broke free from her boot. Shayla's

brain kicked into survival mode masking the pain with adrenaline. She lost a glove, floundering to grab at what she thought was a tree. Chunks of sliding snow, rocks and debris from branches washed downward with her. Shayla tumbled through the dark, searching, struggling, fighting for air.

The slide slowed. She frantically fought to stay with the daylight. As the heavy snow came to a stop, the only part of her body that would move was her right hand. Terror sharpened her perception, and Shayla spastically scooped snow away from her mouth. Adrenaline and fear jolted through in waves of panic. She managed to scoop enough snow from her face, creating a small opening. There was no escape, her movements restricted, she was locked in place.

She screamed toward a small hole of sky. "Help!"

For a split second she was overcome with joyous gratefulness, able to breathe and be alive, but then Shayla was hit by a second wave, a wave of fear.

John.

All of the thoughts of a happy family that flashed before her just moments ago on the chairlift turned to fear. Dreams of a lifetime of love felt lost to fate.

Shayla had stopped praying for divine intervention at fourteen after her father broke through her locked door and beat the hell out of her mother, but without hesitation she prayed now.

Please don't take him. Oh, God, please don't take him. Not now.

Sick fear coiled in her stomach. Her shrilling voice tore through the air as she screamed for him. She couldn't hear anything with snow packed tight around her.

A shadow moved across her speck of sunlight. She heard a muffled voice calling for her.

"John! I'm here!" she cried as the shadow blinded her view of the sky. She felt him digging frantically to free her from the freezing tomb.

The garbled voice became more coherent as the hole got bigger and the snow came away from her ears. "We're gonna get you out. Hold on, lady!"

Lady?

The bitter cold snow cleared from around her head, as a man shoveled desperately around her.

"Where's John? I'm with a man. Where is he?" Her head thrashed as she shrieked. "John!"

"Stay calm. Ski patrol is on the way. We'll find him. I'm going to get you out."

Her arm came completely free and he dug on the other side.

She lay twisted sideways. "Did you see him? Can you hear him? Leave me! Go find him!"

The man's voice remained firm, talking in labored huffs as he dug. "We'll find him."

Shayla heard snowmobiles getting closer. Commands and orders yelled between several men and a woman. *Where did you last see him? Over there, get your poles!* The rumble of the engines started and they took off down the hill, toward the trees, flanking the run they were getting ready to take.

"Go find him! Leave me! Save him!" she shrieked. Hysteria frayed at the edge of her voice. Frustration turned to desperation as she wept small cries of fear. "Please! Please, go help them. I can dig myself out! I need him."

"The sun is going down and I've got to get you out of here before you go into hypothermia."

Her vision blurred with freezing wetness, all she could see was the flash of his red jacket, each time he shoveled. His voice remained flat. "You need to stay calm. You're bleeding from somewhere. Where do you hurt?"

Her mind slowed. Red snow fanned behind him as he shoveled. She tried to process and locate any pain. There was no pain, only numbness. She shook her head.

Another snowmobiler arrived on scene and he began digging around her. Shayla recognized him from the bottom of the hill. She reached for him, but searing pain shot through her left arm. Shayla wailed in agony, cradling her arm. Her heart worked in frantic beats. The echo pounded in her eardrums, robbing her of sound.

"My name is Scotty. We're gonna get you to the hospital. You've got a compound fracture. What's your name?"

"Shayla Clemmins."

Overcome with fatigue and weakness, her pulse slowed. They freed her from the snow, but her limbs wouldn't work. Within seconds the arm of her jacket was cut off and a splint covered her left arm. They strapped her to a toboggan and covered her with blankets.

"I know you. Call JC." Shayla pleaded in a hushed voice as they worked over her methodically. "The girl you were talking to…at the bottom of the hill…it's her brother. Please call her."

He took her pulse. Scotty scanned her face. She saw a muscle twitch near his eye. "What's his name?"

"John Mathews. Call her please."

He gave a quick nod. "I'll call her on the way

down."

CHAPTER FOURTEEN

Shayla didn't remember much of the ride, only the smell of fuel from the snowmobiles and the bitter cold claiming stake to her body. An ambulance waited, and so did Tracy and JC.

Light headed and dizzy, Shayla slipped in and out of consciousness, only able too make out bits and pieces of the conversation. She heard the words *she's in shock* and *we're still looking*.

Fearing the worst, Shayla sobbed in anguish. "I'm so sorry. I told him to go."

Tracy came to her side as the paramedic took her blood pressure.

"I couldn't get my strap on. He was trying to help me." She swallowed against the nausea.

"Don't you dare. Don't you dare think like that, Shayla. He needs you to stay strong right now." Tracy got right in her face. Her eyes welled with fierce devotion for her brother. Tracy's hot tears dripped on Shayla's face, stinging her freezing cheeks. "My brother loves you more than life itself. All he cares about, right now at this very minute, while he's buried under the snow, is if you're alive!"

Shayla nodded, her head listing against Tracy's as to hug her. "I'm so scared."

"Don't you dare give up on him. He needs to

come home."

"You're right. I know he'll make it." Shayla's mouth trembled. "He has to come home. We're getting married."

"He mentioned it a dozen times." JC appeared at her side, forcing a smile through tears of utter devastation. "My brother won't let you down. Ever. He's alive. They're going to find him in time. I just know it."

The paramedic ushered them out, slipping an oxygen mask over her nose and mouth.

Tracy backed away, climbing out of the ambulance.

JC took her place for a brief moment, her eyes glimmering with wetness. She spoke to her real quietly, like a small child. "He's alive. I can feel it. But you need to *believe* it, Shay. You need to talk to him," — JC tapped her temple — "in here. Talk to him. I know he'll hear you and he needs you right now. Let him know you're alive. Tell him to fight."

JC was pulled from her sight.

The ambulance doors slammed shut, and so did her eyes. Consumed with agony and pain, Shayla slipped into shock. Pictures of John's face floated through her consciousness like a wave of water. The memories of John's laughter mixed with the sound of garbled voices and beeping monitors. Shayla drifted in and out of awareness, drugged by the morphine dripping through her veins. She was coherent enough to answer questions the nurses and doctors asked, but she talked to John as if he were right there in front of her. Shayla told him how much she loved him and needed him. She dreamed of their future. The scent of his skin drifted into the bitter taste of antiseptic.

****

"Do you want more ice chips?" came a soft female voice.

Shayla's eyes clamped shut, heavy from sedation. She nodded and opened her mouth. The light touch of icy fingers coasted down her arm. The crunch of is ice fused with a constant beep of monitors.

"Can you open your eyes?"

Shayla's throat hurt when she swallowed. Her mouth felt dry like sandpaper. "More?"

"You can't have too many, you might throw up again," Tracy warned, slipping a few small chips of ice into her mouth.

A wave a panic hit her, accelerating her heart rate. She swatted at the bed in distress. "John? Where is he?"

"I'm right here, baby."

"Am I dreaming?" Her lids flickered drowsily. She licked at her parched lips, trying to make them moist. Her eyes parted in slits, but only saw Tracy. "Where is he? I just heard him, didn't I?"

"He's in the bed next to yours." Tracy offered her a half of spoonful of cold water.

"Hold on. I'm coming." John groaned.

Shayla couldn't move her head, but she heard the crinkle of a plastic mattress as he maneuvered off his bed. "Hi, baby."

JC entered the room. "Hey, she's up again."

Shayla stared at them blankly, foggy from pain meds.

John stepped into her peripheral view, and her eyes opened wide. Her lip quivered as she caught a glimpse of him. "I'm not dreaming, am I?"

John limped to the foot of her bed, dragging his

IV stand, wearing a matching blue hospital gown. He looked scraped, bruised and tired. His warm, rough hand gripped her foot, squeezing and manipulating the arch as he waited for Tracy to get out of his way.

Tracy set the styrofoam cup on the table tray, leading JC out of the room.

He moved to her side, folding his hand over hers. "I'm not a dream. I'm right here."

Shayla's chest felt tight and full. Tears of distress and relief leaked out of her eyes. She tried to sit up, but John gestured for her to stay put as he used the controller to slightly raise her bed.

"Thank God you're alive. I didn't know if…"

"Shh it's okay."

He took a measurable amount of time adjusting into a sitting position at the edge of her bed. Even in her state of drug-induced euphoria, she saw he was in a lot of pain, but she reached for him, needing to touch him.

His eyes were bloodshot and swollen. He kissed her soft and slow, acting as if she were a piece of fragile glass. "I'm fine, baby. Just banged up with a few broken ribs. You're the one we were worried about. You hit your head pretty good and your arm's busted up. You've got two plates and eleven screws in it, but the infection is under control now. Do you remember talking to me earlier?"

"No. Was I awake?"

"I'm not sure awake would be the right word, but you've talked a couple times." His hands never left her skin, caressing as if he needed to touch her as much as she needed to feel him.

"What happened? Where were you?"

"I got tangled at the base of a tree halfway through the slide. The way my body got curled around the tree trunk left a gap in the snow and gave me extra space for air."

She couldn't wait another second. "I love you."

A dark shadow etched across his face and he gripped her fingers tighter. He choked, fighting back a round of tears, but it was no use. They streamed down his face. John chewed on his lip. "I didn't think I was ever gonna see you again, Shay. I love you."

Hindered by painkillers and a broken arm, Shayla stroked his face with her right hand, scratching her fingers through his beard.

He bent carefully, and the taste of salt and medication filled their gentle kisses.

"Does my uncle know?"

"Oh, yeah." John glanced around the room and Shayla's eyes followed his. Three gorgeous bouquets of flowers filled a table.

"I remember smelling flowers."

"My mom and Tom should be here soon, and they made sure you got the best care until they could be here themselves. We're in a private room, and everyone talks about your doctor like she's the best thing since sliced bread. And the nurses jump on command when she walks in the room." John stretched, gingerly reaching for her cup to feed her more ice chips. "We've both had around the clock care with private nurses. They constantly take our temperature and blood pressure, and I've been offered assistance in the shower about half a dozen times."

"I bet you have. Nurses are probably lined up outside the door waiting for you to push the call button." She squinted, moving her finger in a circle over his crotch. "This is mine."

A small grin tugged at the corner of his mouth.

John placed her hand over his heart. "Everything I am, everything I have, every breath I take, belongs to you."

Her chin crumpled. She jiggled his fingers and nodded. "A lifetimes worth."

He searched her eyes. "You remember...everything, don't you?"

A weak laugh wisped from her lips as her eyes drifted shut. "I remember. Don't think you're getting out of marrying me, John Mathews. You're stuck with me forever."

She felt his breath near her temple. "Forever."

Her brows knit as she sifted through her memories. "Was there a dog in here or did I dream that?"

"That's Cindy. You'll meet her. She's part of the ski patrol." She felt him a tremor run through him. "That dog saved my life."

In the middle of the night, Shayla woke up crying, gasping for air, and screaming his name.

John came to her bed and carefully eased in beside her.

Shayla lay nestled tight in the crook of his arm, releasing a shaky sigh of contentment. Her injured arm lay high across his chest on a pillow, and her leg hitched up over his hips.

He smoothed back her hair and kissed her forehead, stroking the tension from her spine. "It's okay. Shh. I'm right here."

Lying in his arms, meshed together as one, the magnitude of nearly losing him overwhelmed her. Shayla wept in the darkness.

His subtle caresses urged her closer into his chest. But it wasn't close enough.

"It's okay, baby," he murmured.

She arched and nudged, needing more of a

connection. Words couldn't convey the amount of love she carried in her heart for this man. She wanted more, needed more.

John's body turned warm beneath her, his arousal growing below her leg.

Shayla maneuvered over him, straddling his hips being mindful not to hurt his ribs. She touched his face in the dark. John's hands roamed over her hips and thighs. He laid the heel of his palm over her heart. She lowered her hand to his chest, feeling his beating heart. She lifted her hips and eased down onto him.

They didn't make love for pleasure. The intimate act went beyond needs and words. They connected as one in a bond of love that that would last a lifetime.

EPILOGUE

Everyone gathered for breakfast at John and Shayla's home in Las Vegas. They'd gotten married the night before at an intimate ceremony at The Little Chapel of Love, and they were leaving that afternoon to enjoy a short honeymoon on the beach in Hawaii.

John and Shayla had searched a total of two days for a new home when Tess called to inform them that she knew of the perfect house, the home John had been raised in.

"Do you think they'll notice?"

"I'm not sure. I don't think so. Well — "

"JC," they said simultaneously.

"She's the master of April fools pranks." John simmered a laugh, rolling his hand over her belly.

Shayla laid her hand on top of his, following the circle. "It's your fault," she teased.

"Me?" He pointed to himself, scoffing in innocence. "The hospital was your fault."

She blushed, but raised her brow, giving him a doubtful smile.

"Okay. The Ranch Exit on the drive home was my fault."

Still unconvinced, she cleared her throat.

"Okay, maybe it was the second Ranch Exit. That one I will proudly take full responsibility for."

He laughed.

They strolled down the long hallway filled with family photos. John stopped to straighten a frame. The wall had just been repainted a creamy white, but Shayla insisted each picture be put back in its exact place. She loved the stories he told recanting each memory of his childhood, captured forever in a photo. Carrying on the family tradition, she'd already added several new pictures.

Their family gathered in the kitchen.

"We have a few pictures we wanted to share with you." John handed his mom a small stack of photos.

"Are these ultrasound pictures?" Tess's blue eyes beamed and a surprised smile broadened across her face.

Tracy and JC quickly moved in around her.

"Yes. We wanted to surprise you." Bliss rang in Shayla's shaky voice.

John wrapped his strong arms around her from behind, pulling her into his chest as he leaned against the kitchen counter. He kissed and nibbled on a sensitive spot behind her ear.

Tess released a small gasp of joy, handing the first photo to Tom. Tracy and JC took the second one.

"Awe. It's a boy!" Tracy exclaimed. "Richard! Awe…you're gonna name him after Dad? Congratulations!"

More squeals of excitement followed from JC. "Can somebody tell me what's what? Wait a minute, this one says Thomas."

Shayla's eyes and nose stung as she watched a veil of pride wash over her uncle's face. They shared a warm smile between them.

"So is he gonna be Richard Thomas Mathews or

Thomas Richard Mathews?"

John and Shayla twisted to face each other. John kissed her cheek and rubbed her belly, a routine becoming habitual. "You tell them."

Shayla lifted her chin proudly. "It's Thomas *and* Richard."

"Twins?" Rang in unison throughout the kitchen.

"Hold on. Wait a minute!" JC squinted at her brother suspiciously. "Is this an April Fools joke?"

For the past twenty-one years, Beverly Preston has been a stay at home mom, although she prefers the title Domestic Engineer, raising her four amazing kids. Along the way, Beverly worked side by side with her husband Don, the love of her life, designing, building and selling custom homes. As her children begin to venture out on their own, she's left to shed a tear—for a minute—wonder what's next in life, and embrace the feeling of empowerment that surely must've been wrapped in a present she received on her fortieth birthday.

If Beverly isn't at home riding her spin bike, you'll find her spinning richly emotional and sinfully sexy romance stories.

www.beverlypreston.com

Made in the USA
Charleston, SC
28 June 2013